Storm!

Dark clouds gather over the township of Storm, Montana. Fast guns have congregated to test their skills against the gun-fighter called Red Rivers. The prize is ten thousand dollars, and Big Kev Riordan needs someone to collect it, because Rivers killed his son and now is the time for revenge.

Into the maelstrom ride two men. One on a blue roan with murder in its eye, the other, on a chocolate-coloured appaloosa. They are said to be wilder than a Texas twister, and tougher than the granite-faced mountains which surround the town. Their names are Josh Ford and Laramie Davis; the marshal and the Legend.

But when the clouds break over the town, the only thing they rain is lead.

Storm!

Sam Clancy

A Black Horse Western

ROBERT HALE

ISBN 978-0-7198-3049-5

The Crowood Press
The Stable Block
Crowood Lane
Ramsbury
Marlborough
Wiltshire SN8 2HR

www.bhwesterns.com

Robert Hale is an imprint
of The Crowood Press

This one is for Sam and Jacob

Typeset by
Derek Doyle & Associates, Shaw Heath
Printed and bound in Great Britain by
4Bind Ltd, Stevenage, SG1 2XT

PART 1

DARK CLOUDS GATHER

CHAPTER 1

Rivers watched them enter. His brown-eyed stare drilled out from underneath the brim of his black hat and followed them across the smoke-filled saloon. Three men. No, two men and a kid. But to the gunfighter, it was clear that the thin-faced stripling was in charge.

All were dressed in suits and wore bowler hats. They paused when they found a table that suited their needs, and stared at the two men and the scant-ily-clad whore who sat there.

Standing a touch over six feet, Clay 'Red' Rivers was solid-built. He had dark hair and a week's growth of stubble adorned his face. At his right thigh a Colt Peacemaker .45 rested in a black-leather gun rig, the same color as his clothing. 'Who are they?' he asked the woman who was sitting across from him.

The blonde turned to glance over her shoulder. It took only a heartbeat for her to recognize them and she turned back to Rivers, wide-eyed.

'It's him. Oh, Christ, he's back.'

Rivers frowned. 'Who is he, Violet?'

'I got to go, Red. Before he sees me.' The whore gulped down the last of her drink and started to rise from her seat.

'Who is he?' Rivers asked again.

'Johnny Riordan,' she blurted out and hurried toward the stairs.

'Who the hell is Johnny Riordan?' Rivers muttered to himself and poured another drink.

A man pushed in through the doors from the lamplit boardwalk and scanned the room. He too wore a suit, and when he saw the others, crossed over to them. When he sat down at the table, his black coat fell open and Rivers saw the shoulder holster beneath it and the small six-gun nestled inside.

The man happened to glance across and saw that Rivers was looking at him. He must have said something to the others at the table, because they did the same and then looked away dismissively.

Rivers was happy about that. The last thing he wanted was trouble. He'd had enough of it over the past year.

The gunfighter had arrived in the township of Carter's Bend, Kansas earlier that day. It was the second time he'd been to the town, hence the reason he knew Violet, and that she worked in the Sly Dog Saloon.

In fact, most of the town knew who he was but they left him alone. The last time he'd been there he'd killed a man who had thought his skill sufficient to beat Red Rivers on the draw for killing his brother.

One of the men at the table rose from his seat and walked across to the long wooden bar with the polished top and waited for the barkeep. While he stood there, Rivers noticed him looking into the big rectangular mirror which hung above a row of bottles. The gunfighter figured the man was scanning the bar. Which might betray him as a professional.

Rivers watched on as the barkeep walked along the bar and stopped in front of the man. They exchanged a few words and then the barkeep pointed across to the table where Rivers sat.

Reaching under the table, the gunfighter flipped the hammer-thong off the Peacemaker and rested his hand on the butt.

The man then walked back the way he'd come, bypassed the table where he had been seated with the others, and continued towards Rivers' table. When he reached it, he stopped and stared at the gunfighter.

'The barkeep said you might know where Violet is, since she was drinking with you?' he said,

Rivers held his gaze. 'I might.'

The man's brows knitted together. 'Well?'

'Well what?'

'Where is she?'

'I don't know.'

'You must know. She was drinking with you.'

Rivers nodded in the direction of the table from whence he come. 'Who is the kid?'

'What's that got to do with it?' the man snapped.

'Just curious.'

'He's none of your damned business,' the man snarled.

'He your boss?'

'Maybe.'

Rivers nodded. 'He someone important?'

'Why?'

'Figured he must be since he has the three of you riding shotgun on him.'

There was movement as the young man rose from his chair and started to walk towards them.

'Here comes your boss,' Rivers said.

Up close the young man looked even younger. He had fair skin and peach fuzz on his face.

'Wells,' he said, 'What is the problem? Have you found out where she is yet?'

The man called Wells shook his head. 'No, Mr Riordan.'

'Well, why are you standing here?'

He pointed at Rivers. 'The barkeep said he might know where she is since he was the one drinking with her,' Wells explained.

Riordan eyed Rivers with caution and then asked, 'Do you know where she is?'

'I don't think she wants to see you, kid,' Rivers told him.

'Why do you say that?'

'She took one look at you and ran in the opposite direction.'

Riordan looked like he was put out by the inconvenience of having to find Violet for himself.

'Which way did she go?'

9

'Why don't you just leave her be?' Rivers suggested. 'It's obvious that she's scared of you.'

'I'll be the judge of that. Now, which way did she go?'

'Don't know.'

Riordan's face changed colour as a tinge of red crept across it.

'I don't think you know who you're talking to, mister, so I'll let it go. My name is Johnny Riordan. My father is Big Kev Riordan, from St Louis.'

'Is that supposed to mean something to me?' Rivers asked.

'It will possibly be the last name you ever learn before you get planted if you're not careful, Mr. . . ?'

'Rivers, Red Rivers,' the gunfighter supplied.

'I'll give you exactly ten seconds to tell me what I want to know, Rivers, or my man, Wells here, will shoot you dead.'

Rivers shifted his gaze to Wells. 'I know you know who I am, Wells. But it's obvious that the kid don't. Now, just so you know: if you make a move toward that shoulder holster I'll kill you.'

The kid snorted in disgust at what he considered an empty threat. Rivers looked at him and said, 'Under this table I have a Colt Peacemaker. It's pointed at your man's guts. By the time it blows through the tabletop and reaches him it will be all bent out of shape. Make an ugly wound that he'll never recover from.'

Wells licked his lips. 'Take it easy, Rivers, I ain't going to draw on you.'

10

'You'll do what I tell you to, Wells,' the kid persisted.

'Listen, Johnny,' Wells grated. 'There are times and places for this type of thing. This ain't one of them. I'll go and look for her if you want, but I ain't pulling on Rivers.'

Young Riordan gave him a look of disdain. 'How do you know he ain't lying?'

'I don't. But I'm not crazy enough to find out.'

The kid stared at Rivers before he hissed, 'This isn't over, Rivers. You've made a big mistake.'

He turned on his heel and stalked off across the room followed by Wells. The gunfighter already knew he was going to have to kill that one before he got killed.

Violet was scared. After going upstairs in the saloon, she'd taken the back stairs down into the alley. From there she hurried to the small one-room cabin she called home. It was normal for the girls from the saloon to sleep in the rooms they entertained in, but Violet was the exception.

She sat down at the small table and stared at her shaking hands. Clasping them together she tried desperately to make them stop. Maybe she should have stayed there with Rivers. If Johnny had tried to start something, maybe the gunfighter would have killed him.

'Stupid,' she hissed. 'You should have stayed.'

Tears welled in her pale-blue eyes. Why wouldn't the spoilt little bastard just die? He needed to. He needed to die before he could hurt anyone else. Images came into Violet's mind of the last time Riordan had beat her. She'd been laid up for a week, battered and bruised, cracked ribs, one eye shut. But no one had done anything about it. Not one man had raised a finger to help.

An idea came to Violet and she rose from her chair and crossed to a shelf where an old tin sat. Lifting it down, she removed the lid and emptied the contents onto the table next to the lamp the coins rattling, and proceeded to count the money.

Fifty dollars. That was all she'd managed to save. Would it be enough? Would Rivers kill him for that amount? She scooped the money back up. God, she hoped so.

Violet hurried to the door and swung it wide. She had to get back to Rivers and offer him the money. She was about to step through the opening when four men appeared in front of her. She pulled up short and paled. Johnny Riordan smiled at her.

'Hello, Violet. Have you been avoiding me?'

CHAPTER 2

'If that bitch is still asleep I'll give her a piece of my mind,' Honey growled as she hurried toward Violet's cabin. 'I can't understand why she can't blame-well sleep at the saloon like the rest of us.'

It was a little after nine in the morning and the Kansas sun was well above the eastern horizon. It was a condition of the girls' employment that every morning they helped to clean before the saloon opened. Even if they'd been up most of the previous night with customers. So, when Violet didn't show, Ernie, the barkeep and saloon owner, sent blonde-haired Honey to fetch her 'skinny ass' back there.

And what made the situation worse was that Honey had stood in horse shit on the way over. 'Frigging lazy bitch,' she cursed as she remembered it.

Honey walked up to the door and shouted, 'Violet! Ernie said to get your skinny ass over to the saloon right now or you can forget about working Saturday night!'

There was no answer and Honey clenched her right hand into a fist. She lifted it to shoulder height and then pounded on the door with it. 'Violet! Viol. . . !'

The door swung gently open and Honey stared at it. She shrugged her shoulders and called out as she stepped through the door 'I'm coming in, Violet, and you better be awake!'

A few heartbeats later an ear-piercing shriek sounded.

When Rivers awoke that morning he figured that it was a good day. He stood at the second-floor window and looked out at the townsfolk passing below. From there he'd gotten dressed, had a large breakfast of ham and eggs, washed it down with coffee, and went along to the telegraph office to see if the wire he was waiting on had arrived.

It hadn't but the telegrapher told him that it would probably be another couple of hours away.

When he was on his way back along the boardwalk he saw a small crowd of men carrying something across the street. Behind them he recognized two of the whores from the saloon; both seemed to be crying.

When he got closer to the group he realized what it was the men were carrying. A person. A female. When he saw the bloodstained blonde hair hanging limp his blood ran cold.

Rivers hurried along the boardwalk to close the distance between them. When he reached the group he could see that it was Violet, despite all the bruises and blood which covered her face.

'What happened?' he snapped, hoping for an answer.

'Someone all but killed her,' a man said as they walked past. As they disappeared into the doctor's office Rivers grabbed Honey by the arm.

'Who did this?'

Him being a shade over six-one, Honey had to look up. With tear-filled eyes, she sobbed, 'It was him.'

'Who?'

'Him who done it before.'

'The kid?'

She nodded. 'Only this time it's worse. This time she could die.'

'Did she say it was him?'

'How could she? You saw her. But it was him. I'm sure of it.'

Honey shook free of his hand and followed the others into the office. Rivers turned to look out at the street and the crowd which had followed the small group with their gazes. He couldn't see the men he wanted anywhere.

He ought to go looking for them but knew that if he found them he would end up killing one or all of them, and as yet they hadn't been identified as the ones who'd done it. That would be up to Violet if she ever woke up. So he'd wait. If they left town in the meantime, he'd track them down. It didn't matter. If they were guilty, then they would pay.

*

Rivers sat on the dusty boardwalk steps and waited. He saw the noonday sun come and go, likewise various townsfolk. A little after two in the afternoon, Honey emerged. Rivers stood up from where he'd been keeping his vigil and studied her face. She looked tired, her face was drawn.

'How is she?'

The whore looked at Rivers and tears came to her eyes as the shock wore off. 'She died. She's dead. I can't believe it.'

She collapsed forward into Rivers' arms. The dam wall within her burst and the tears flooded out. Rivers felt her sadness flow from her body and remained silent while she wept. Then she drew back.

'She died, but not before she said who killed her. It was him. Johnny Riordan.'

Rivers eased her away from him and stepped back. She studied his face and could see he was up to something.

'What are you doing?'

'I'm going to find him.'

'But there's four of them.'

'Yeah, there is that, but I'll be fine.'

'They'll kill you,' Honey said, alarmed.

'I doubt it. Go and tell the sheriff what you know. Maybe he'll get there in time to help out.'

As Rivers started to leave, Honey called after him.

'Stay alive, Red.'

*

He caught up with them in the saloon. They were laughing, seated around a table, unaware of the storm coming their way. When Rivers found them they had no idea that the woman had died. All that was about to change.

It was Wells who saw Rivers coming, and the look on his face was enough to make him do something stupid. He went for his gun.

Rivers' right hand blurred and came up with a roaring .45. The lead slammed into the man's chest and knocked him backward over his chair, out of sight.

The two others snapped their gazes toward the gunfighter, jaws dropping in shock at the sudden and violent death of their comrade. Riordan stared at the still-smoking Peacemaker, voice full of bravado, and said, 'You're a dead man, Rivers.'

'Says the pot calling the kettle black,' Rivers sneered.

'What?'

'In other words, I'm here to kill you, kid,' the gun-fighter explained. 'Violet died.'

Riordan's face remained passive as the words descended like a pall of smoke blanketing the room. Through the silence a voice from behind Rivers said, 'I got me a shotgun lined up on you, Red. Just let the hammer down on that hogleg and put it away.'

A spark showed in Riordan's eye. He smiled and said, 'I hope you're here to arrest this man for murder, sheriff?'

'I'm here to arrest someone for murder,' the sheriff

said, 'but it ain't Rivers. It's you, Riordan. Violet woke up long enough to name you as her killer.'

'That's horseshit,' Riordan hissed.

'Hand over your gun,' the sheriff said.

'Come and get it.'

A murmur rippled through the gathered crowd. Then footsteps sounded on floorboards. Rivers watched as the sheriff walked past and approached the table. The gunfighter grew alarmed when the lawman blocked his view, placing himself directly between killer and gunfighter.

'Give me the gun, Johnny.'

'Sure, Sheriff. Anything you say.'

A gunshot sounded and the sheriff stiffened. He went up on his toes and teetered there for a moment before falling to the floor. Rivers cursed. He side-stepped to clear his line of sight after the shot had been fired, then brought the Peacemaker into line. He thumbed back the hammer and centered the barrel on the kid's chest.

He caught the look of grim excitement on Riordan's face and knew he'd have to kill the kid. It was the only way. Johnny Riordan saw that the gun-fighter held the gun aimed at him. His expression changed with the sudden realization that his time had come to an end.

The slug from Rivers' Colt erupted from the barrel with a roar and punched into Riordan's chest. The kid's gun spilled from his hand and Rivers shifted his aim to cover the remainder of the newly deceased's entourage.

'Make your play if you've a mind,' the gunfighter offered. Neither of them moved. Rivers nodded.

'Then take your dead and get the hell out of town.'

The two men who stood before Big Kev Riordan feared for their lives – and were right to do so. After all, they'd let the boss's kid get killed.

'How did it happen?'

They told him about the whore and the sheriff, and then about the gunfighter named Red Rivers.

'Who is this Red Rivers?' Big Kev asked.

The man cut an imposing figure. He was over six feet tall, broad-shouldered, and had a solid, square jaw. But most of all he exuded a power that came from being a killer. He felt no compunction when it came to ridding himself of those he disliked, usually by the hands of others following his orders. However, he was not averse to getting his own hands dirty.

Most people in St Louis knew him as a businessman. The exception to that was the law, who knew exactly what he was. Sure, there had been whispers, but no one ever voiced their opinion too loudly.

When they didn't answer he snapped, 'Well? Who is he?'

'He's a gunfighter, like we said,' one of them ventured.

Big Kev's eyes narrowed. 'I know that, Rich. Tell me something I don't know. Like where the hell I can find the bastard?'

The man named Rich shrugged. The other one,

named Porter, spoke.

'He's good, Kev. Has to be. Wells was scared of him.'

That was enough to give Big Kev Riordan pause. He'd never known Wells to be afraid of anyone. Then he brushed it off.

'If he's so good, then why haven't I ever heard of him?'

The answer was a simple one. Big Kev was always so wrapped up in his own little world that not much else filtered through. But they weren't about to tell him that.

'He's never been to St Louis before,' Porter said. 'But word is that he's the best there's ever been for a long while.'

Big Kev nodded thoughtfully. 'Where's my boy?'

'He's at the funeral parlor.'

Big Kev nodded again, then turned away from the men. They could barely contain their surprise and relief that he hadn't killed them. Instead, he spoke clearly so there would be no mistake about what he was saying.

'Come and see me tomorrow. I will have a list of names, and I want you to find each and every one and have them come to Storm, Montana.'

Rich raised his eyebrows. 'Storm, Montana?'

'Yes. Are you hard of hearing?'

'No, boss. What shall we tell them?'

'You'll tell them that they'll have a chance to earn ten thousand dollars.'

Both men were taken aback by the statement.

Their jaws dropped at the mention of such an exorbitant sum of money.

'Don't just stand there gawping. Get the hell out of here before I change my mind and shoot you both for letting my boy get killed.'

Hurriedly they put their hats back on and disappeared out the door.

Big Kev turned to the other man in the room. One who'd remained seated and silent throughout the whole exchange. He was a slim Chinese man who went by the name of Li Chin.

'Can you find this Rivers?' Big Kev asked him.

The Chinese man nodded. 'Yes.'

'I don't want him dead. He must be alive when you get him.'

'I can do it,' Li Chin said.

'Good. When you do, take him to where I said.'

'What is there?' Li Chin asked.

'A town. Not much of one. The last time I was there it was all but a ghoster. But the best part about it is what isn't there. Law. There's no law for a hundred miles in any direction.'

'What are you going to do?' Li Chin asked.

'We're going to have ourselves a little carnival. And Red Rivers will be our guest of honour.'

CHAPTER 3

Gentleman Jim Brown finished trimming his pencil-thin moustache in the fly-shit-marked mirror and replaced the scissors in their leather folder. It was a ritual that he followed on the mornings of the days he planned to kill someone. On this day the distinguished honour would go to Flash Pete Murray, another killer of class.

It was a well-anticipated duel. Since the arrival of both men in Compton, Kansas, the buzz throughout the small town had not been 'if', but rather 'when' the two famed gunmen would face off.

Brown placed the folder in his small bag which held other personal items. He then reached for the light-coloured, leather holster in which rested a nickel-plated Colt with mother-of-pearl grips. He strapped the belt around his slim hips, adjusted it and took his coat from the bed.

Putting it on, he studied himself in the mirror. *Looking good, Jim. Looking good*, he told himself.

The gunfighter left his room and locked the door

behind him. He walked along the hallway to the top of the stairs and stared down into the barroom below. One by one those below noticed him and suddenly the room was quiet.

Brown commenced his slow descent, his footfalls sounding deafening in the silence. When he reached the bottom he paused yet again, allowing the tension and drama of the moment to build. He walked along the bar and the other drinkers before him parted to reveal Flash Pete Murray at the far end, dressed in his usual suit of clothes. The gunfighter looked up at Brown and nodded. 'Buy you a drink, Jim?'

Brown smiled. 'Sure, why not?'

Murray said to the nervous-looking barkeep, 'Get the man a glass.'

'Yes, sir,' came the reply. A few moments later the glass was on the scarred counter, waiting to be filled.

Murray did the honours and moved the drink along the bar to Brown.

'There you are, Jim. Enjoy.'

'Thanks, Pete.'

They each finished their drinks and turned the glasses upside down.

'Are we going to do this outside on the street, Pete?' Jim asked Murray. 'Be a shame if one of the good townsfolk stopped a bullet if we did it in here.'

'Probably be best, Jim,' Murray agreed. 'Meet you out there.'

Brown watched Murray go through the doors, then looked up at himself in the mirror. At forty he was considered an old man in his profession. He often wondered how many of these encounters he had left in him. He guessed that he'd find out eventually.

Following Murray out, Brown stopped on the boardwalk. His gaze ran left and right along the street. Word had spread that this was the day the two would fight it out. Townsfolk lined each side of the street, the atmosphere charged with anticipation.

Stepping out onto the hard-packed dirt of the street, Brown paused. He closed his eyes and looked up. Feeling the sun on his face he breathed deeply through his nose, savouring the aroma of the plains as it swept along the main street.

Opening his eyes, he turned to face Murray who stood no further than twenty feet from him. Pulling back the flap of his coat, he revealed the butt of his six-gun. He nodded. 'Whenever you're ready.'

There was a pregnant pause while both men eyed one another and then after what seemed like an age, Murray moved.

His hand streaked towards his gun butt, clawing at the grips, polished over time by frequent use. His weapon had just started to come free of the holster on his hip when the first slug from Brown's Colt slapped into his chest, the sound of the shot lost in the roar of the crowd as it rolled along the street.

Casually, Brown dropped the Colt back into its holster while Murray stood there, mouth agape, a large red blossom on his chest growing bigger with every second he remained erect.

It wasn't until Gentleman Jim turned away from

him that his legs finally gave out and he fell into the dirt and shit of the street. The violent life of Flash Pete Murray was finally over.

'Mr Brown?'

Brown stopped and watched as a thin man in a suit and bowler hat stepped down from the boardwalk. The man approached him and stopped. 'What do you want?' Brown asked.

'I have an offer for you, Mr Brown.'

'Not interested,' the gunfighter said, shaking his head.

The man hesitated, then spoke in a low voice, 'It's worth ten thousand dollars, Mr Brown.' The flicker in Brown's eye told the man he was hooked.

'Who do I have to kill?'

'Red Rivers.'

Tentative fingers gripped the edge of the ramshackle counter as the man cowering behind it pulled himself slowly to his feet. Great beads of sweat had formed on his brow, his eyes were rolling wildly with fear. The stench of gun smoke seemed to scorch the inside of his nostrils while his ears still rang from the furious rattle of gunfire which had recently stopped.

'Are – are they dead?' he stammered.

Scar Fletcher looked around the dim interior of the trading post at the four downed men. One of them moaned and the bounty hunter raised his Schofield and put a bullet in the man's head.

'They are now,' he growled, his voice low and gravelly. 'Get me a drink.'

The trader, a man named Peters, fumbled with a bottle of watered-down rye and poured the liquid into a glass.

'Th – there.'

Fletcher placed his now empty sawn-off shotgun on the counter and the Schofield beside it. He took the glass then raised and emptied it in one gulp. He slammed it back down.

'Again!' he snapped.

While the trader poured another drink with a shaky hand, Fletcher rubbed at the puckered scar on his left cheek, from which he'd gained his name. It was courtesy of a bullet from Lefty Wilson, a small-time outlaw. Alas, Lefty was no more.

The second drink hit the counter and Fletcher helped it on its way. Peters looked nervously at him and asked, 'Another?'

'No. Give me a hand to get them on their horses.'

'What about the other one?' Peters asked.

'What other one?'

'You mean you don't know?'

Fletcher stared hard at the trader. 'I've a feeling you're going to tell me.'

'There were five of them. The fifth one left here yesterday and I heard him say he'd be back today.'

'Jenkins was only supposed to have four in his gang,' Fletcher said. 'Where'd he get the fifth from?'

The trader shrugged. 'He met them here.'

It made sense, Fletcher supposed. He'd followed Jenkins into the Nations from Kansas and there'd only been four of them then. Their trail had led him here, Peter's Trading Post in the middle of nowhere.

'Do you know what the other feller looked like?'

Peters nodded. 'Tall, thin. Long hair, buck teeth, and a face on him like a mule's ass.'

'Uh huh. You know what they called him?'

'Chapman, I think.'

Fletcher smiled. 'I guess I'm about to make me some more money today, then.'

'Who – who is he?'

'They, not he. I've a feeling that when Chapman returns, he'll have others with him. Namely French Burton.'

Peters paled. Burton was worse than Jenkins ever had been. It was obvious they were to meet and join forces. For what, Fletcher didn't care. All that mattered was there would be money at the end of it for him. More than the two thousand dollars he currently stood to make.

In the waning heat of the late afternoon, three riders came in from the east. Out back, the corpses were already ripening where they lay behind the stalls. Inside the trading post, Fletcher sat next to the window, waiting for them to arrive. His sawn-off shotgun was loaded once more, as was the Schofield. He swallowed the last of his drink and came to his feet.

Peters automatically dropped behind the counter.

'Relax, I ain't going to shoot them in here.'

The reassurance didn't help and Peters stayed

where he was.

The riders were just pulling up out front when the door opened and Fletcher walked out to meet them. He stood there, shotgun in his left hand, the Schofield in his right. His steely gaze settled on Burton.

'Howdy, Frenchy,' he said.

'Is that you under that black hat, Scar Fletcher?'

'You know it is.'

'I thought it was, given the state of your clothes. You're about the only feller I know who bathes once a year and still smells like death.'

'Is that right?'

'I don't suppose you've seen Jenkins around here at all?'

Fletcher nodded. 'I did.'

Burton shifted nervously in his saddle. 'Where is he, then?'

The bounty hunter made note of the other two riders spreading out.

'He's out back with the rest of them. You'll be joining them directly.'

'You sound mighty confident, Scar.'

'Just facts, Frenchy.'

A gust of wind blew in from the west and stirred the parched dust into a small cloud. It flung the grit at the mounts ridden by the outlaws, causing them to throw their heads in the air. It was all the distraction Fletcher needed and he took full advantage of it.

The shotgun came up and roared a throaty chal-lenge. Its charge of buckshot shredded the shirt of the rider on the left, turning his chest to a red mush. He was flung back over the rear of his horse and the animal spooked. It jumped to its right, whirled, and then took off.

Fletcher's right fist bucked as the Schofield fired shortly after, the slug punching through the forehead of the outlaw on the right, his head snapping back as the top was blown right off.

It all happened so fast that French Burton, a hardened killer, froze. The Schofield moved slightly as it lined up on him. Fletcher smiled.

'I guess you're about to have a bad day, Frenchy.'

'Wait—'

The six-gun spat lead and the slug hammered into Burton's chest. He straightened in the saddle, fighting to stay erect. A second bullet ended that battle and he fell from his horse with a dull thump, throwing up a puff of dust as he hit the hard-packed earth at his mount's feet.

Fletcher walked forward and checked to make sure they were all dead. Behind him, he heard the door to the trading post open.

Peters stepped out into the last remnants of sunlight, looking down at the fresh corpses before swallowing quickly, then asking, 'Is it over?'

Fletcher nodded. 'Yeah.'

By the time Scar Fletcher rode into Brooks, Kansas, with his macabre caravan, the bodies had more than just a slight stink to them. Townsfolk stopped and stared at the unkempt rider leading the string of corpse-laden horses, then they got the whiff of putre-fying flesh and their noses wrinkled at the offensive smell.

Brooks wasn't an overly large town but was quite central for Fletcher, so it was the place he brought most of his corpses for the rewards. Sure, at times there were closer towns, but the bounty hunter, for some strange reason, seemed to prefer to bring them here. Maybe it was the fact that it pissed the sheriff off.

He eased his horse up to the hitch rail outside the jail and dismounted. As he went to step up onto the boardwalk Sheriff Joe Morris appeared in the doorway, an undisguised look of disgust on his face.

'Christ, Fletcher! I should've known it was you. I could smell you coming along the damned street.'

Fletcher smiled at the large man. 'They are a little ripe, ain't they?'

'Who is it this time?'

'Jenkins and his boys and French Burton and his.'

'You've been busy.'

'Yeah,' Fletcher said and went to step up onto the boardwalk as before.

'No, you don't, Scar. You smell just as bad as they do. Get them over to the undertaker and have your-self a damned bath. I'll organize everything that needs to be done. Come and see me then.'

Fletcher shrugged and said, 'OK then. I'll be back in a couple of hours.'

'Make it tomorrow. It'll take all of that time to get the stink off you. And one more thing. There was a feller in town looking for you. Been here the best part of a week. I think he's still here. Ain't seen him leave yet.'

'What's his name?'

'Rich or something like that. Wears a suit. I warned him it might be best to steer clear of you less'n he wants to get some of your stink on him. Guess he wants to see you real bad.'

'The question is, Morris, what about?'

The sound of footfalls stopping outside his door made Fletcher's eyes snap open. His right arm came clear of the lukewarm water and dropped to the floor beside the tin bath. His fingers wrapped around the butt of the Schofield and he thumbed the hammer back. The triple-click was almost deafening in the still room.

Using his tongue, Fletcher moved the cigarillo from one corner of his mouth to the other. Then he waited.

The knock at the door was followed by the door swinging open. A man stepped into the room and saw the bounty hunter in the tub, a gun pointed in his direction. 'You won't be needing that.'

'Who are you, and what do you want?' Fletcher demanded. 'And why couldn't it wait until I was out of the tub?'

'My name is Rich. I'm here on behalf of Big Kev Riordan.'

'Is he a feller I should know?'

'I don't know. Do you?'

31

'Never heard of him,' Fletcher growled. 'Keep talking.'

'It seems he's heard of you. He wants to offer you the chance to earn ten thousand dollars.'

The expression on Fletcher's face changed and he asked the same question that Jim Brown had, 'Who do I have to kill?'

'Red Rivers.'

CHAPTER 4

Two-Gun George Butler was fast. Not as fast as some, people would say, but in his mind, there were none better. He sat in the corner of the dusty cantina waiting for Frank Garza to come in for his afternoon drink.

Garza was the son of a Mexican and a gringo whore. He was a hired gun wanted north of the border for killing a town marshal. But that wasn't why the tall gunman was here – here being a one-horse peon village just across the border in Mexico.

Butler sipped his tequila and placed the glass back down on the scarred tabletop. He slapped at an annoying insect which was trying to bite him on the skin of his exposed neck, and muttered a curse. He hated coming to Mexico, no matter how well he was being paid to take out the killer.

Scratching his boots on the dirt floor, Butler picked up the bottle and topped up his glass. A little prostitute with long dark hair and olive skin saw him sitting by himself and walked over to him.

'You want some company, *señor?*'

He gave her a half smile. 'Sure, why not?'

She hurried away and grabbed herself a glass from the rough-looking counter where a fat Mexican stood wiping dust from every surface. She sat down and pushed the vessel across for Butler to fill.

'What's your name?' he asked her.

'Conchita. What is yours?'

'George.'

'What are you doing here, George?'

'I came to kill a man.'

If he was hoping to shock her, he was wrong. Instead, Conchita shrugged her shoulders and said, 'Maybe he will kill you.'

'I doubt it.'

She sipped her drink and pulled a face. 'This tastes like horse shit in it.'

'Complain to your boss.'

'I might have to.'

There was movement in the doorway and a man wearing a suit walked in. Butler watched him cross to the bar and talk to the Mexican.

'You want to come out the back with me, George?'

'I'm waiting for someone. I told you.'

She smiled knowingly. 'He will not be here for another couple of hours yet.'

Butler's eyes narrowed. 'Who won't be?'

'Frank Garza.'

'How do you know that it's him I'm after?'

'It is always the same. At least Conchita can make the last couple of hours of your life more pleasant.'

'You assume that I will be the one killed.'

Conchita nodded. 'As I said, it is always the same.'

The man at the bar turned and started to walk in Butler's direction. The gunfighter stiffened and drew his right-side Colt. Thumbing back the hammer he kept it hidden below the table. The man stopped.

'Are you Two-Gun George Butler?'

Butler nodded. 'I am.'

'You're a hard man to catch up to. My name is Porter. I have come to discuss business with you on behalf of Big Kev Riordan.'

Butler stood up letting the man see his Colt.

'It'll have to wait. The little lady and I have a previous engagement. Help yourself to a drink.'

Conchita came to her feet and the gunfighter said, 'Lead the way, little darling.'

Porter watched them disappear through a curtained doorway at the back of the cantina. He looked around the room and saw the other customers drinking lazily, not a care in the world. He shrugged and sat in Butler's seat, filled the empty glass and took a hit.

An hour later Butler lay in the lumpy-mattressed cot with Conchita's head resting on his left shoulder. He had to admit, she was like a stick of dynamite under the covers and if he *was* to die this day, it would be with a smile on his face. But that wasn't about to happen.

A fly buzzed about the room and he tried to find it with his eyes. He scratched his nose and let his right hand drop down. Not far away from it was a chair on which lay his Colt, well within reach.

'Why do you do it?' Conchita asked.

'Do what?'

'Kill men.'

'I guess it's something I'm good at.'

Conchita rose up and stared into his eyes, her long dark hair falling across his chest. 'Aren't you afraid you will be killed?'

'The thought never entered my head,' he said.

Conchita was about to say something else when the door of the lean-to was flung open with a crash. A man filled the door, a Winchester in his hands. Butler caught a glimpse of the weapon and wrapped his left arm around a startled Conchita, pinning her to him like a shield.

The Winchester roared and Butler felt the whore shudder under the bullet strike. The shooter levered again and fired. The second shot followed the first and ripped into the petite body atop the gunfighter.

The naked Butler rolled to his right, releasing the body of the whore as he fell off the edge of the cot to the floor. Scrambling for the Colt, his fingers found it as a curse was followed by another shot. The confined space was filled with a roar and the bullet bit into the wellworn mattress.

The gunfighter brought his Colt up and snapped off a shot. The lead burned into the shooter's left shoulder and brought forth an immense cry of pain. Butler fired again and this time the slug flew true, punching into the killer's head. Blood and brains sprayed in a dark mass across the wall behind him, then the killer dropped to the floor, dead.

Butler came to his feet and checked the fallen man. It was Garza. He shrugged and turned back to look at the blood-soaked cot where Conchita lay. Her eyes were open in death; fear etched on her face, the last emotion she'd felt. The gunfighter said, 'Thanks for your help.'

No one came, whether from fear or just ignoring the gunshots, he'd wasn't sure. But Butler dressed and left the lean-to and went inside the cantina.

The man called Porter was still there waiting for him. Butler sat down and poured himself a drink into the glass Conchita had used.

'What was the shooting?' Porter asked.

'Business transaction.'

Porter nodded. 'Speaking of business, do you have time to talk now?'

'All the time in the world.'

'Good. Let's talk about Red Rivers.'

'What about him?' Butler asked curiously.

'My boss is offering you a chance to kill him.'

'How much is he paying?'

'Ten thousand.'

The second glass of tequila stopped halfway to the gunfighter's mouth. 'Ten thousand?'

'Yes.'

'You expect me to believe that?'

'Like I said, Mr Butler. It is only a chance. There are others who are getting the same offer.'

There was no decision to be made. Butler said, 'I'm in.'

'Good. You need to go to Storm, Montana. Once there you will wait until things are ready. Provided you make it in time.'

'I'll make it all right.'

'Good. We'll see you there.'

Porter got up from the table and walked toward the doorway. Watching him go, Butler smiled. *Ten thousand dollars*. That sure as hell was some payday, and he sure as shit aimed to collect.

There were still two names on the list that had to be contacted. One was a young man, not much more than a kid. The other was an old campaigner, as dangerous as they came. The kid was said to be in Colorado. The other, Montana.

But it was the kid who was up next. He was called Jimmy the Kid. A name which he'd given himself out of sheer cocky arrogance. He thought he was invincible. And to some who saw his lightning-fast draw, they probably thought so too. Except for Grunt Caldwell. Caldwell thought him a two-bit punk who had no respect for anyone. And he was probably right. However, that didn't count for much. Caldwell was going to show him that respect for your betters was sometimes earned the hard way.

The hard-headed gunfighter rode into High Ridge, Colorado on a tired-looking bay. He'd travelled almost a hundred hard miles to get there after he'd heard about the Kid killing Bunt Craig.

The way the witnesses told it, the Kid had waited until Craig had his gun halfway out of leather before he started to draw. And the gunfighter still hadn't been able to get off a shot before the Kid killed him.

Caldwell cried bullshit over this. There was no way some punk kid could get the best of Craig, especially when he was that far behind. To top it off, the Kid had shot him three more times even though he was dead. Two of those bullets had blown off the index finger of each hand. Craig's trigger fingers.

So, Caldwell had put out the word. He was coming for the Kid to teach him some respect of his own. That day had come.

And so had the spectators. Word had spread like a California wildfire and now they all lined the street with anticipation of what was about to happen.

A third of the way along the town's main street a grey-headed man stepped from the crowd lining the boardwalk. He had a star pinned to his shirt. Caldwell eased his mount to a stop when the lawman moved to block his path.

'You have no business here,' the sheriff said. 'Turn your horse around and leave.'

Caldwell ran his gaze over the crowd on both sides. A voice shouted from somewhere on the left, 'Let him go, Vince. Be the most exciting thing to happen 'round here in a long time.'

The gunfighter gave the sheriff a cold smile, 'Can't let the folks down now, can I?'

Vince stared at him for what seemed an age before stepping aside. Caldwell nodded. 'I knew you'd see it my way.'

Once more, his horse moved forward. The man

who'd called out to the sheriff to leave Caldwell be shouted out once more. 'He's in the Sunrise Saloon!'

The crowd moved like a wave along the board-walks, both sides, not wanting to lose sight of the gunman or miss anything.

Caldwell saw the saloon coming up on his right. Once again the horse came to a stop. The gunfighter dismounted and led the animal across to the hitch rail. He tied it off and stepped back out into the middle of the street.

'Somebody go tell that upstart son of a bitch I'm here to kill him.'

The saloon batwings were slowly pushed open and a middle-aged man slipped tentatively into the room. He glanced around and saw Jimmy sitting at a table with a woman in her early forties, dressed in a low-cut, emerald-green gown. The man cleared his throat and said, 'He – he's here, Jimmy. Grunt Caldwell is outside on the street.'

Jimmy wasn't just a kid by name. He *was* a kid. Seventeen and looked every bit his age. He sighed and glanced at the woman who sat across the table from him.

'Guess I got to go, Ruby.'

'Damn it, Jimmy. I told you to quit calling me that.'

'Sure, Ma.'

'That's better.'

Ruby wasn't just any whore. The Kid had grown up around the tough men and saloon harlots his entire life. The bawdy women had looked after him, the hard men and killers taught him about life. His father had given him only one thing before he left when Jimmy was a baby; his gun speed.

Jimmy stood up and adjusted his Colt in the holster set up for a right-handed cross-draw. He picked up his bowler hat from the tabletop and placed it on his head, covering the red hair he'd inherited from his mother.

'Be careful, Jimmy,' she said to him as he leaned down to kiss her on the cheek. 'You're too young to die.'

'It's a good thing I'm too fast to die then too, huh, Ma?' he smiled at her and his pale blue eyes sparkled. From where his mother sat, he looked just like a freckle-faced kid. The thing was, this kid had a barb in his tail which gave off a wicked sting.

He started towards the batwings. When he reached them, Jimmy paused. Pushing out through them and onto the boardwalk, he left his mother sitting there wondering whether this would be the last time her son would walk away from her.

CHAPTER 5

The crowd gave a cheer when they saw the well-dressed Jimmy emerge and step from the planks of the boardwalk and onto the street. With steady, confident paces, he walked to the middle of the thoroughfare and turned to face Caldwell.

The gunfighter spit in the street and sneered, 'Shit. You ain't much more than a sprout. How you ever bested a man like Bunt Craig I'll never figure.'

'He was just too slow,' Jimmy said innocently. Caldwell's eyes narrowed, angry at the slight.

'The hell he was. Craig was one of the fastest guns there's been.'

'And yet he's dead,' Jimmy retorted. 'Go figure.'

'Why did you do it?'

'Do what?'

'You know what I mean, you little punk,' Caldwell snarled. 'Why'd you shoot his trigger fingers off?'

'Because he didn't need them anymore.'

A chuckle rippled through the crowd, and

Caldwell spat in the dirt at his feet again.

'Smartass, huh?'

Jimmy ran his gaze over the man before him.

'Mr Caldwell,' he said, 'I'm feeling awfully generous today. How about we forget about this and go and have a drink. That way you can stay alive and . . .' The kid searched for some words. In the end, he just shrugged and said, 'Well, you can stay alive.'

Caldwell couldn't believe what he was hearing. Who was this little bastard to speak to him this way? He flexed his fingers as they hovered above his gun butt. He could feel the anger towards the kid burning deep within him. The time for talking was done.

'Are you ready, Kid?'

'Are you?'

A heavy silence descended upon the street and tension started to build at the unanswered question on everyone's lips. *Who would die today? The Kid, or Caldwell?*

Somewhere the silence was shattered by the slam of a door. Both men reacted to it and hands dove for their guns. Caldwell was fast. Real fast and he knew this one was one of his best. But it wasn't good enough to match the Kid.

Jimmy's Colt was clear of leather well before Caldwell's. The hammer was back and the finger starting to depress the trigger. Only one shot rocked the main street. The Kid's.

Caldwell felt the hammer blow in his chest and staggered. When he looked down and saw the rapidly-spreading red stain, he glanced back up, his mouth agape. The Kid stood there, no more than twenty feet away, smoking six-gun in his hand.

The dying gunfighter gave a bewildered look, still unable to comprehend how the Kid had bested him. Then he fell like a cut tree to the street and didn't move.

The cheer that rose along the street was almost deafening. Nearly everyone who'd watched it happen with a macabre fascination had their arms in the air. Jimmy smiled at them and turned to go back into the saloon. He stopped and then waved for them to follow.

They all let out another cheer, and like the wave that had followed Caldwell along the street when he rode in, they did the same to Jimmy.

'*All hail the prince*!' the half-drunk man shouted as he patted Jimmy on the shoulder.

Jimmy turned to face him as uproar went through the packed saloon. He waited for the noise to die down and said, 'What do you mean, *Prince*, Buck? I would have thought at least *king*.'

The middle-aged man smiled. 'There's only room for one king at the top, Jimmy. At the moment that man is Red Rivers.'

Jimmy nodded and smiled. Ruby, on the other hand, could see the anger in his eyes at the mention of the name Red Rivers. For a good while now, the Kid had been harbouring the need to face down the man they called the best. Every time someone discussed the very name, a dark cloud seemed to appear behind Jimmy's eyes.

He glanced at Ruby and saw the worried expression on her face. Nodding at her, he gave a small smile, trying to allay her fears.

Just then a man pushed through the crowd. He stopped in front of Jimmy and said, 'Might I have a word with you?'

'What about?' Jimmy asked.

Buck said to him, 'Go away. 'We're celebrating.'

'What about?' Jimmy asked again.

'I'd rather tell you in private.'

The Kid smiled at him. 'These people are all my friends. I keep no secrets from them.'

'It is a chance for you to earn yourself ten thousand dollars.' The man had to shout to be heard.

And heard he was. The entire room went silent. Jimmy couldn't stop his face from showing amazement at such a sum. What he could do with that amount of money was beyond belief. He glanced at Ruby and saw the fear in her eyes. She shook her head.

'Jimmy, no.'

Shifting his gaze, he stared at the stranger and asked the same question as the others before him.

'Who do I have to kill?'

'Red Rivers.'

Laramie Davis drew his chocolate-coloured appaloosa to a halt on the rocky ridge and looked down on the town below. He removed his dark hat and ran a hand through his collar-length brown hair and reminded himself that he needed to see a barber. The same went for the covering of whiskers on his tanned face. Behind him, the horse he had on the lead had stopped too.

'What are we stopping for?' its rider growled.

Laramie turned in the saddle, the early morning sun catching the nickel-plated marshal's badge pinned to his chest and making it flash.

'How about you keep that lip of yours buttoned, Mako.'

'My damned leg is damned well hurting from that damned slug you put in it, Laramie. I need to see the damned doctor down there in Trent.'

'Maybe next time you'll think twice about pulling a gun on me then,' Laramie growled.

'Maybe next time I won't miss,' Mako hissed.

'And maybe next time I'll just kill you. Now shut the hell up.'

Mako cursed under his breath and said no more.

At forty-five, Laramie had seen a lot in his travels across the West. The one-time gunfighter had recently pinned the badge on again to work for an old friend.

He shifted his solidly built six-foot-two frame in the saddle. Boy, was he ever looking forward to a bed for the evening! Although it was still early, he decided to stop over in Trent for a meal, a barber, and a soft bed. Plus, Mako did need to see a doctor about his wound.

About Laramie's waist was a brace of Colts; he was

quite proficient in their use and had proved so on more than one occasion.

His horse, Bo, shifted beneath him, wanting his rider to keep moving. Laramie leaned forward and patted his neck.

'Easy, feller. We'll get there.'

Bo moved forward off the rise and down the slope toward the town. Behind Laramie, Mako started to complain again.

'Damn horse this, damn horse that. Why the hell did you have to shoot me?' and other general horse-shit.

By the time they reached the edge of town, Laramie was really starting to wish he'd killed him. He swore that his ears were about to bleed from the pounding they had received from the constant yabbering.

The street was a bustling hive of activity and the strangers to town drew more than their fair share of attention. Laramie found the jail and helped Mako off his horse. He was about to climb onto the boardwalk when the sheriff appeared. A thin man with sandy-coloured hair, he took one look at the badge Laramie wore and said,

'What can I do for you, Marshal?'

'The name's Davis. I'd like to put my prisoner up for the day and the night if that's OK with you?'

'Sure. My name is Crown. Who's he?'

'Mako Henderson.'

Crown nodded. 'He don't look like much.'

'Even less with the bullet I put in him. He'll need

a doctor.'

'I'll get one of my deputies to fetch him.'

'Thanks, appreciate it,' Laramie said. 'Come on, Mako, inside.'

'Damn it, Laramie, I. . . .'

'And for Christ sakes, shut the hell up.'

Laramie put Bo and the horse Mako was riding up at the livery and went back to the jail. The doctor had already checked over the outlaw and recommended a few day's bedrest. Laramie nodded and said that it wouldn't happen; they were riding on the next day for Helena.

Next Laramie found himself a place to stay for the night. It was a small hotel with a limited amount of rooms. Once he was squared away, he decided that a drink was in order and found the Penny Dreadful Saloon. Buying a bottle, he then found a table in a quiet corner of the room and relaxed.

While sipping his whiskey, he scanned the room, taking in his surroundings. He came to the conclusion that it wasn't the worst saloon he'd ever been in but it was far from the best. Picking up the bottle to pour himself a third glass, it happened. It always happened. Though less frequently these days. Almost all the men who wanted him dead were in the ground. Except for Cletus Burns. And wouldn't you know it, the son of a bitch walked right into the saloon and looked straight at Laramie.

Crossing the room to where Laramie sat, Burns gave him a cold stare.

'Someone said you was wearing a badge again. Too bad it won't damn well help you.'

'Why are you here, Cletus?'

'You damned well know why I'm here,' he snarled. 'You killed my brother.'

'He drew first, Cletus. He'd have killed me if I hadn't shot him.'

'It don't matter much. I'm still going to kill you.'

The barroom had gone quiet, all eyes on the two men. Laramie shook his head. 'Turn around and leave, Cletus. No good can come from this. Especially for you.'

'Stand up, Davis, or I'll shoot you where you sit.'

'I ain't standing up, Cletus.'

A mask of rage covered the would-be killer's face.

'Last chance, Davis. Get up!'

'No.'

'Then die where you are, you son of a bitch!'

Cletus's hand flashed down for his weapon. Fingers wrapped around the gun butt and that was as far as he got. The tabletop exploded as Laramie discharged the Colt hidden below it. Wicked splinters scythed through the air and lacerated the exposed flesh of the killer's face.

But that was the least of his problems. The flattened hunk of lead ripped into his chest and made a horrific mess of everything it touched. Cletus staggered under the bullet's impact. His mouth worked overtime as he tried to draw air into his lungs but nothing seemed to work. Eventually, he dropped to the floor, his weakened legs unable to support him any longer.

Laramie got to his feet, gun smoke still rising from the Colt's muzzle. The sound of the gunshot had died away and all that could be heard in the eerie silence was the liquor spilling from the overturned bottle of whiskey.

Two days after the gunfight in the saloon, Laramie arrived in Helena with his prisoner. He locked him up and gave his report to the marshal in charge. Since Bass was taking time away from the job, that just happened to be Roy Willis.

Once he was finished there, he took care of Bo and then walked along to the hotel where he usually stayed. Collecting the key for his room, he trudged slowly up the stairs, weary from the long ride. *Getting old is for the birds,* he thought. He was just about to the top when his path was blocked by a stranger.

Laramie raised his tired head and stared at him. The man gave him half a smile and asked, 'Are you Laramie Davis?'

Alert now, the gunfighter eyed the man cautiously, waiting for any sign of trouble. 'What if I am?'

'Could I talk to you about something? It's a private matter which could earn you quite a sum of money.'

Laramie kept up the steps and stopped on the landing.

'I don't use my gun for profit anymore, Mr—'

'Rich. I work for Big Kev Riordan. Have you heard of him?'

'Nope.'

'He is in need of a gunman – a few gunmen actually

– and is offering ten thousand dollars to the man who can complete the task which is set.'

'As I said, I don't do that anymore.'

'Not even for ten thousand?'

'Who is it?'

'Red Rivers.'

Laramie nodded, glad his badge was covered by his coat. He'd heard of him. Some said he was good; others, the best.

'Why?'

'The boss figures he has it coming.'

'So, all I have to do is kill him?'

'Basically. But it's not quite that simple. There will be a gathering of guns in a place called Storm. Are you familiar with it?'

'I am,' said Laramie.

'Everyone is to meet there. Other gunmen will be present for their chance to collect. The first one to kill Rivers gets the money.'

'I thought Storm was all but a ghost town?'

'It is, but Big Kev is spending some money. It's going to be like a carnival.'

'When?'

'Two weeks. Are you in?'

'If I am, I'll be there.'

Rich smiled. 'Well, hopefully, we'll see you there.'

Roy Willis was in the middle of paperwork when Laramie returned to the office. He looked up and gave him a puzzled look.

'I didn't expect you back here until tomorrow.'

Roy Willis was a slim, thin-faced man with more than his fair share of years as a deputy marshal. Hence why he found himself sitting behind a desk filling in for his boss.

'I think we may have a problem in a little town called Storm.'

Willis frowned. 'Storm? I think I've heard of the place. Trouble, you say?'

Laramie explained about his visit from the man called Rich and the offer of big money for him to go to Storm and participate in the spectacle.

'Two weeks, Laramie?'

'Yeah.'

'This Big Kev feller must have himself some kind of set against Rivers if he's willing to go all out after him.'

Laramie nodded. 'Red's not the kind of man you want to brace unless you've got a lot of back-up.'

'Is he faster than you?'

'I'd hate to live off the difference.'

'OK. I'll have someone dig around and see what they can come up with. Meanwhile, head over to Silver Bow County and find Josh. He's working on a case over there. Actually, he should have it almost wrapped up. Bring him back here. If there is something going on in Storm, I think it might need two of you.'

'You want me to leave today?'

Willis shook his head. 'No. Josh should be fine until you arrive. As I said, he should almost have it wrapped up.'

CHAPTER 6

At the same time that Laramie was in the marshal's office, Red Rivers was in Payton, Wyoming trying to convince the Bent brothers that they didn't have to die. Especially for a reason he didn't rightly understand.

Chad and Gray Bent came as a duo. If you hired one you got the other. Kind of a two-for-one deal. They were low-life tenth-raters whose ambitions were mixed up with their capabilities. Normally when they came across someone like Rivers, they were more likely to back shoot him rather than face him head-on like they were. And that's what confused Rivers the most.

'Don't look like he's worth that much,' the gap-toothed Chad grumbled.

'Word has it he is,' baldy Gray confirmed.

'You sure they meant him?'

'Sure, I'm sure.'

'What are you two fellers on about?' Rivers snapped, his patience running out.

Chad's face screwed up and he said, 'We aim to kill you.'

It was more like, *we aim to keeeell yoouuu.*

'Why?' asked Rivers.

Gray licked nervously at his scabby lips. He looked around at the gathered crowd watching on from where they stood under the awnings of the false-fronts lining the street.

Gray leaned closer as if someone might overhear him, and he mumbled something. The bystanders had no hope of hearing him because Rivers was only twenty feet away and he heard nothing. He screwed his face up and winced.

'What?'

The outlaw gave him a perplexed look and repeated his mumble.

'Oh for Christ sake, dumbshit, I can't damn well hear you,' Rivers cursed.

' *'Cause you're worth ten thousand dollars*!' Gray shouted and then realized what he'd done. Chad slapped and cussed him.

'You stupid son of a bitch, what you go and shout it for?'

'I couldn't help it. *You* heard, *he's* deaf.'

'He was right,' Chad said.

'What about?'

'You are a dumbshit.'

'Where'd you hear that from?' Rivers asked the brothers.

'Ain't telling,' Gray said, sounding like a petulant child.

54

'*Where*!'

They both jumped. 'The Kid.'

'What kid?'

'Jimmy. Jimmy The Kid.'

'Who the hell is he?'

Chad frowned. 'You ain't heard of him?'

Rivers shook his head. 'Should I?'

'He's the next best thing. The next you. Some say he's faster than you already.'

Gray nodded. 'Yes, sir. He's fast all right.'

'Where did you see this Jimmy?'

'We saw him the other day. Him and a whole heap of folks are headed to Storm.' Gray stopped and frowned. He turned to his brother and said, 'If he's going to Storm to kill Red, how come Red ain't there?'

Chad stared at Rivers. 'How come you ain't there?'

'Where?'

'Storm. Jimmy said he wasn't the only gunfighter to be going that direction. Word is that there's more of them. All after the ten thousand for the man who kills you.'

'Did he say who it was that was paying?'

'Nope.'

'So, you fellers figure you'd cash in early?'

'Yeah.' Chad nodded. Rivers had heard enough.

'Go away and leave me be.'

Gray shook his head. 'No, we aim to collect.'

'No, you don't, you aim to die.'

'We'll just have to see then, won't we?'

For a moment, while he was talking to them,

55

Rivers thought there might be a way out. He was wrong. Although, he didn't want to kill them. They were just too dumb to kill.

'All right, let's get it over and done with.'

In the next instant, the brothers were all business. They separated and went into a crouch.

'You all want to draw first?' Chad asked Rivers.

'No. It wouldn't be fair.'

'Have it your way.'

Hands dropped to gun butts and the brothers commenced their draws. Rivers, however, already had his own gun out and working. Both Bent brothers spun around, guns falling from their hands. They lay in the dirt of the main street, clutching at their wounds, moaning in pain.

Rivers stood over them with his gun in his hand. Gray looked up at him and he said with a pain-wracked voice, 'You shot me.'

'No shit.'

'Shut up, Gray,' Chad growled. 'He shot me too. What makes you so special?'

'You fellers learned your lesson?'

'I guess so.'

'Good. Now get patched up and point your broncs for Mexico,' said Rivers. 'Next time I won't be so for-giving.'

'I'm telling you, there's a whole heap of folks heading to Storm to see this shootout for the ten thousand,' Honey heard the cowhand say.

'I don't believe you,' said his friend.

'It's true. All these gunfighters are headed there to go up against Red Rivers. The prize is all that money. But they have to kill him.'

Honey drew in a sharp breath, worry filling her eyes.

'Why would he do that?' the second man asked.

The first man lowered his voice, but luckily, he was seated right behind the whore.

'Word is he won't have much choice. What do you say? Should we ride on over to Storm and have a look?'

'How are we going to get there? If we ride it'll take forever. It's a long way from Kansas to Montana.'

'We can catch the train. Are you in?'

'Sure, why not?'

Honey rose slowly from her chair. The barkeep called out to her from across the room. She walked over to the bar and before he could say anything, she told him:

'I need some time off.'

He looked at her like she was stupid. 'You what?'

'I need some time off.'

The barkeep snorted. 'The only time off you'll be getting is off your feet. A customer just went upstairs. Go and entertain him.'

Honey glared at him but did as she was told. As she stomped up the stairs, she acknowledged the fact that she wasn't done yet.

'You're crazy, Honey!' Tina exclaimed. 'What could we do against hired guns?'

'I don't know, but don't forget what he did for Violet. He killed the person responsible. It's the least we can do – for us to help him out somehow.'

'You don't even know if he's in trouble,' Cheyenne pointed out.

'He's in trouble, I can feel it.'

'And how do you think we can get there?' Tina asked.

'The train. We can take it so far and then we can buy some horses or a wagon and go the rest of the way.'

'Oh goody. I've never been on a train before,' Clara said, clapping her hands.

'Shut up, Clara,' Tina growled. 'That doesn't help.'

'Leave her alone,' Cheyenne's eyes blazed red, matching her hair.

'Are you coming or not?' Honey asked one last time.

'I am,' Cheyenne said.

'Me too,' said Clara.

Honey stared at Tina; her ample chest was heaving, and she was uncertain if she was making the right decision. She rubbed at her dark hair as though it would magically give her the answer she required.

'Tina. . . .'

'All right! I'll go.'

'Good. The train leaves tomorrow.'

'We'll still need money once we get there,' Clara said. 'How are we going to get that?'

Honey smiled. 'The same way we always do.'

*

Rivers spent the best part of the night lying on his bed, going over in his mind all his enemies who would possibly want him dead. None of them had the kind of money required to set up such a bounty on his head.

So that left the impossible and he didn't have any luck there either. Hell, the last person he'd killed had been the kid in Kansas. That had been a touch over two weeks before. All he could be certain of was that someone wanted him dead and they were paying big dollars to make it happen. But then there was Storm. What did the town have to do with it? He wasn't even there and yet that was where the guns were gathering.

The gunfighter figured he had two choices. He could ride out tomorrow, head for California, and lay low for a while. Or he could ride to Storm and find out what was going on.

When he saddled up and rode out the next morning, his horse was pointed north, toward Montana.

PART 2

FORKED LIGHTNING!

CHAPTER 7

'I'm going to kill you, Marshal! You hear me?'

United States Deputy Marshal Josh Ford sighed and replaced his drink on top of the polished bar. Why was it that everywhere he went, the crazies always followed him? He looked up at the tall barkeep and said, 'It's never easy is it?'

The man gave him a puzzled look. 'Marshal?'

'Never mind.'

Ford picked up his drink again. Maybe if he ignored the dumb shit he might go away.

'Did you hear me, Marshal?'

Nope.

Ford stared into the mirror behind the bar, below which sat three shelves of bottles and glasses. He was in his early thirties, had a solid-built six foot one frame, dark hair, black clothes and hat, and blue eyes which right then were saying, *I've had enough of this horseshit.*

He was in Huntsville following up on a case where someone was stealing gold from miners, sending

61

them broke so that they were forced to sell out to one man. From what he could gather there were two elements involved. Those who were killing and stealing, and the man who was behind the whole operation. He just needed proof. And that was hard to come by.

Now this.

'*If you don't come out, I'm coming in there, Marshal! If I do, I'll be coming shooting!*'

Ford knocked back his drink and turned, placing his back against the bar. Nearly every person in the dimly-lit saloon watched him in anticipation. Was this it? Would he go out there now? Face down Burt Wilson?

No. Instead, Ford drew his Peacemaker and casually checked the loads.

Behind him, the now nervous barkeep asked 'Are you going out there, Marshal? I don't want Wilson coming in here shooting.'

Wilson was a thief. He and his brother Hank had been arrested after they'd robbed a stage and Hank had shot the guard. Ford had been the man who'd found them. Hank was hanged and Burt was sent to the pen for fifteen years. After two of those years he'd escaped and now he was here in Huntsville, Montana. Obviously with vengeance in his heart.

'Marshal?' the barkeep said tentatively.

There was one man in the room, however, who was enjoying every moment of it. A thick-set man with a brooding demeanor. He was the one rooting for the killer. With a little luck, all his problems would end right here, right now. That man was John Carlton, assayer, and the man behind the Silver Bow Gang, as the killers were being called.

'*That's it, Marshal. You've had your chance. Here I come, you son of a bitch!*'

There was a moment of silence as Ford snapped the loading gate shut on his six-gun. Then came the sound of boots thumping across the boardwalk planks. Getting louder, closer. The batwings flung open and . . .

. . . Ford shot Wilson dead centre in his barrel-like chest.

The outlaw was punched back through the batwings by the .45 calibre slug, a red blossom on his chest. He disappeared and the deputy marshal casually holstered his Colt and turned back to the bar.

A buzz began to reverberate around the room. They'd never seen anything like it before. The deputy had just casually shot Wilson who'd been coming through the doorway. No fuss at all.

Carlton was not one to join their excitement. Instead, he walked from the saloon and went back to his office. He would have to figure out his own way of killing the lawman.

His departure didn't go unnoticed. Ford was watching in the mirror and saw him leave. Deep down he knew the man was behind everything that was happening.

The back door of the assay office opened and a tall man with weathered features walked in. He was dressed much like a saddle tramp, only he was more dangerous than one of those could ever be. His name was Spike Connors.

Carlton looked up from his wooden desk and saw him standing there. Alarm was replaced with anger as he hissed, 'What the hell are you doing here? I told you and your boys to stay out of town while that blasted marshal was around.'

Connors shrugged. 'The boys are getting restless. They want something to do instead of sitting around all day staring at cabin walls.'

'Well, I ain't got nothing at the moment. The next gold shipment isn't due to go out until the day after tomorrow. Besides, there's the marshal to think about.'

The outlaw grunted. 'Who is this dang marshal anyway?'

'His name is Ford.'

'Ford?'

'Yes.'

'Josh Ford?'

'That's him.'

Connors smiled coldly. 'I do hope I meet him somewhere along the way. I'd like to swap lead with him.'

The assayer thought for a moment.

'On second thought,' he said, 'I just might have something for you to do.'

'What's that?'

'Kill the damned marshal.'

The outlaw's eyes glittered in anticipation.

'When?'

'Tonight. He's staying at the Sundown Hotel. Second floor, second window along the balcony on Main Street. If you do it, I'll pay you an extra five hundred.'

'I'll do it, all right. He's as good as dead.'

Ford opened the door to the assayer's office and walked inside. He bellied up to the dark wooden counter and saw that the place was empty. Near his hand was a small bell, shaped not unlike one of those seen hanging around the neck of a milk cow. He picked it up, gave it a shake, smiled thoughtfully, then shook the hell out of it until Carlton appeared from another room. He gave Ford an indignant stare and asked brusquely, 'What can I do for you, Marshal?'

'I was hoping I could ask you a few more questions about the claims which were hit and then acquired by yourself.'

'All legitimately I assure you, Marshal. The owners sold to me of their own free will.'

'Maybe . . .'

Carlton smiled.

'. . . Maybe not.'

The smile was gone.

'Do you have a map I can look at?'

Carlton eyed Ford suspiciously. He hesitated and then nodded.

'OK. I can find one.'

A few minutes later the assayer had a map laid out on the counter. It was pale and lined but Ford could make out all the distinguishing features.

'Can you show me where the claims are that were shot up?'

Carlton pointed them out one-by-one. Four of them all in a line.

'Do they pay well?'

'I'm not sure. They're not being worked at the moment.'

A curious expression came to Ford's face. 'You're not sure? But you're the assayer. Surely they brought some ore in here for you to weigh and check over?'

'Well . . . yes, they did. . . .'

'Was it good ore?'

'I suppose.'

'You suppose?'

Carlton was fast becoming frustrated. 'Yes, I suppose.'

'You know what I think?'

'What do you think?'

'I say that there's a rich vein of gold running right through all of these claims here and you knew this and have yourself a scheme to pick them up cheap.'

'That's preposterous!'

Ford's gaze became like granite.

'Is it? You're the right man in the right position to figure it out. You know what else I think? I think you're not done yet. There's at least two more claims out there on that line and you've got your sights fixed right on them.'

'How ridiculous,' Carlton snapped. 'Get the hell out of my office and take your false accusations with you.'

The deputy marshal stared at him in silence just long enough to make the assayer uncomfortable, then he said, 'All right. But I've got me a feeling I'll be back.'

Beneath his breath, the assayer mumbled, 'Don't count on it.'

CHAPTER 8

Red had a feeling that there was someone on his backtrail. Although he hadn't laid eyes on them he knew they were there. He'd been sensing it for the past two days. Stirring the fire with a stick, making the flames leap higher into the air, he placed a blackened coffee pot over the heat provided and waited for it to boil.

Somewhere to the north, a coyote let out a mournful howl, while to the west the last pink hues of sunset were almost gone. The sudden nickering of his horse had Rivers dropping his hand to the butt of his Colt.

A twig cracked and the six-gun came free of leather.

'Don't shoot,' a man's voice said. 'I'm friendly.'

'Come in nice and slow.'

A shadow loomed up from the darkness as the man walked into the orange glow of the firelight.

'You can put the gun away if you want.'

'I'll be the judge of that. My name is Clay Rivers. Who are you?'

'My name is Li Chin. Pleased to meet you, Clay Rivers.'

Rivers' head felt like someone was inside it with a blacksmith's hammer and pounding hell out of it. His body rocked from side to side as the ground lurched beneath him.

The ground don't lurch.

He opened his eyes and was blinded by the brightness of the sun. He closed them again and listened intently to his surroundings. Hoofbeats, the grind of steel-rimmed wheels. He opened his eyes again and this time he saw the bars. Vertical. Solid.

'I see you are awake,' the voice said.

Rivers looked through the bars and saw a rider on a horse. Li Chin.

'What's going on?' the gunfighter asked.

'This wagon will be your new home for a little while. Until we get where we are going.'

Wagon? Rivers looked around once more. He was in a wagon. A tumbleweed wagon. There was a driver on the seat and another man beside him.

'Where are we going?'

'To Storm.'

It was late when a shadow crept along the balcony toward the window of Ford's room. It was an hour or so after midnight and the street was quiet. The saloons were closed, such was the rule on a weekday, which the sheriff enforced. Hence, there was no one around to see the following events unfold.

Connors had climbed up to the hotel balcony using the awning post. Once over the railing, he sneaked along the balcony until he was next to the window of Ford's room. The darkness made the killer's smile invisible as he contemplated what he was about to do.

Stepping in front of the window, he rammed his six-gun forward, the barrel smashing the glass, and started firing.

It wasn't until the gun ran dry and bullets began to come back at him that he realized he'd missed.

Now he was in real trouble.

Ford was suddenly awake. He lay there quietly as he tried to figure out why. He listened for noise in the hall but there was nothing. Then he thought that maybe it was something from the street below which had filtered up.

Wrong again.

Then what could it be?

He saw the shadow on the balcony about the time that the window shattered, and the gun started to fire. The muzzle flash lit up the room and Ford heard the first slugs start to burrow into the wall behind the bed. As agile as a cat, he rolled off the bed and onto the floor. Bullets thudded into the mattress and blew stuffing into the air.

As suddenly as the shooting had started, it stopped and Ford was able to grab his Colt from the nightstand. He fired two fast shots at the window and heard boots hammering on the boards. The shooter was running away.

Not wanting to get glass in his feet, he pulled his boots onto stockingless feet, grabbed his gun belt, tossing it over his shoulder and headed for the door.

Ford took the stairs two at a time and ran through the foyer. He unlocked the heavy entrance door and opened it. The moonlight afforded him a glimpse of the shooter about to disappear into an alley.

Two more shots rang out from Ford's Peacemaker and he made a mental note that he only had two left.

The slugs ripped splinters from the corner of the building next to the alley. Ford chased after the shooter, cursing that he'd missed.

He turned the corner and was confronted with the Stygian darkness of the alley. The shooter could be in there somewhere and he'd not know it until he fell over him. Unlike himself right now, silhouetted against the mouth of it.

Ford ducked back and listened. Hearing footsteps running away, he moved back around the corner and into the alley. Hoping there was nothing below knee level that he could trip over, he started to jog.

However, Ford was too late. The shooter's horse had been tied out the back, and the man was already mounted and riding away. The deputy fired his last two shots after the rapidly-disappearing figure and, once again, they both missed.

'Son of a bitch,' he hissed, then turned and started to walk back to the hotel.

CHAPTER 9

Gentleman Jim Brown was the first to arrive in Storm. He rode in early the morning after Connors had tried to shoot Ford in Huntsville. Dressed immaculately as usual, he eased his horse to a halt outside the Big Sky Hotel.

He shook his head and said, 'This isn't quite what one expected.'

The hotel was in a shocking state of disrepair. One of the windows was broken, the door was hanging off, and the sign that hung from the awning was only attached by one corner. And this was one of the better buildings in the town.

Storm had once been a thriving centre surrounded by timber-clad hills which led up to great grey, granite-faced peaks that, come winter, would be covered in a thick fall of pure-white snow. Between two such peaks was a waterfall that cascaded into a deep gorge; and like everything else in the colder months, it iced over, creating a magnificent sight in Storm's background.

'Which one are you?' a voice asked from the balcony.

Brown looked up and saw a big man there flanked by another.

'I'm Jim Brown. You might call me Gentleman Jim.'

'Good. I'm Big Kev.'

'Ah yes. "The Financier". Where might I find the guest of honour? Might as well get it over and done with.'

A gust of wind blew along the street and stirred up some of the finer dust particles.

'He's not here yet. Although I have it on good authority he'll be here in a week or so.'

'Damned inconvenient.'

'Not if you're the one who wins the money.'

Brown nodded. 'Where might I find a place to sleep in this rat-infested hole?'

'Here's as good a place as any. I have a team arriving tomorrow to fix the place up ready for our big event.'

The gunfighter screwed up his nose.

'The only way to get a place like this ready would be to burn it down.'

Big Kev chuckled. 'You know, you just might be right.'

Brown climbed the steps and walked through the doorway into the hotel. The foyer was covered in dust and broken items. He walked over to the counter and found a small bell. When he picked it up the handle came away. The gunman snorted derisively and shook his head.

He turned away and walked over to the stairs. He scrutinized them intently before placing any weight on the first step: he thought it best to be cautious, remembering the way the bell's handle had come away.

As he began to ascend, the treads seemed to moan their protest at his passage.

'I say again, this is most inconvenient,' he said.

Laramie rode into Bucheron late in a haze-filled afternoon. Somewhere north of the town a large fire burned, staining the sky with a thick brown smudge. He figured he'd reach Huntsville sometime the following day.

Bucheron was a ten-year-old timber town built around a lumber camp by folks who'd seen a need. Now it was a thriving little centre constructed entirely from local trees. False-fronted shops lined the main street, their large façades hiding the smaller structures behind.

The deputy marshal found a place to put Bo up for the night, then wandered along the boardwalk until he found a hotel that looked to be reasonable. He entered the lobby and walked across to the counter.

A young lady was dusting the polished wooden top and looked up when he said,'Would you have a room, please, Miss?'

She gave him an apologetic smile: 'I'm sorry, sir, but we're full.'

Laramie nodded. 'Is there another hotel I might try?'

Again, that same apologetic smile. 'I'm afraid everyone is in the same circumstance. Ever since the crowd came into town.'

'Big crowd, huh?'

'Yes. Rowdy too. They say they're headed to Storm. Lord knows why. It's nothing but a ghost town these days.'

Laramie had an idea why.

'I guess I can sleep over at the livery. I'm sure he wouldn't mind the extra money. Thanks all the same.'

'I'm sorry.'

Laramie walked back to the livery. He found Mort the hostler, a thick-set man who wore overalls.

'Do you mind if I sleep in the stall with my horse?' Laramie asked.

'Everything full up, huh?'

'You could say that.'

'I'll do you one better. I've an empty stall down the far end. I'll put some fresh straw in it for you and I won't let it out.'

Laramie smiled and dug into his pocket for some money. Mort shook his head.

'Don't worry about it. One night won't send me broke.' The deputy marshal nodded.

'I was going to find a meal. My things . . .'

Mort held up a hand.

'I have an office up the front. Put it in there while you're gone. I'm here until late anyway.'

'Thanks.'

Bucheron seemed to take on a life of its own after dark. Once the sun had retired for the day the streets came alive with excitement. At a small café run by an elderly couple, Laramie had just finished a thick stew with potatoes, and after paying left and was walking towards the Bow and Arrow Saloon.

Men and women, more than a good percentage of them well on the way to being drunk, spilled from the saloon and out onto the well-lit street in a giant wave that made the deputy marshal wonder if there was anyone left on the inside.

They seemed to be gathered around a young man, a kid would probably be a more accurate description, who as far as he could figure, was the source of their excitement. Laramie spoke to a man leaning against an awning post.

'What's happening?'

'Young Jimmy is going to show us some of his fancy shooting.'

Looking around the crowd, Laramie saw a familiar face. A woman. He walked over to where she stood and said, 'Hello, Ruby.'

At first, her face was a mask of curiosity as she looked to see who was talking to her. Then her face changed, and fear replaced every emotion.

'Laramie? What are you doing here?'

'Just passing through, Ruby. It's been a while.'

'You need to leave,' she blurted out, panic in her voice. 'Go before he sees you.'

Laramie was confused. 'Before who sees me?'

'Jimmy.'

'Why should that worry you? He's only putting on a show for the folks. He—' then Laramie saw the red hair in the light. 'He's your son.'

'Yes, he is.'

'Well, little Jimmy is all growed up. But why should that concern me?'

'Because you're Laramie Davis, that's why!' she hissed vehemently.

The deputy marshal was about to say something when a slim-built man beside him, with a voice that sounded like fingernails being run down a chalk-board, asked, 'You're Laramie Davis?'

'No,' Laramie snapped.

But the ugly-faced man didn't listen.

'Hey, it's Laramie Davis.'

The raucous crowd went silent and turned as one, searching eyes looking for the famous gunfighter. Ruby placed a trembling hand on Laramie's arm.

'Leave, please. Before he sees you.'

But it was too far gone for that. As he turned, Laramie heard the voice say, 'Where are you going, Mr Legend?'

Laramie's blood ran cold, as it always did at hearing the name. He glanced at Ruby and saw her shake her head. She mouthed the word, *Please*.

The deputy marshal took a step to keep going but the voice sneered, 'Are you running away?'

Laramie turned to face the kid.

'I'm a little old for games, kid,' he said. 'Plus it's

past my bedtime.'

Ruby seemed to relax a little at his words, but the kid was like a dog with a bone.

'Come on, Davis. It's all in the name of fun.'

It's never about fun. 'All right, kid. What is it you want to do?'

A cheer went up and the deputy marshal tried to give Ruby a reassuring look. He stepped down onto the street.

'What are we doing?' he asked.

'How about a test of gun speed?'

Laramie hesitated.

'No? Don't want to participate in a friendly test of . . .' the kid searched for the word, then instead said, 'Afraid you've slowed down in your old age?'

A ripple of laughter ran through the crowd at the jibe. Laramie gave a half-smile at the kid's attempt to bait him.

'All right, kid, what are we shooting at?'

'Each other.'

'Jimmy, no!' Ruby gasped.

Jimmy saw the troubled expression on Laramie's face and laughed.

'I'm just joking. How about we put some bottles in the street and use those?'

The deputy marshal nodded.

'I'll get some, Jimmy,' a man shouted and disappeared into the saloon.

'There are a lot of stories about you, Davis,' the kid said. 'Are they all true?'

'The ones about my death ain't.'

78

Jimmy smiled. 'You're funny. I like a good sense of humour.'

And you're a boy playing in a man's world. 'What I'm saying is don't believe everything you hear.'

There was movement as the crowd parted to allow the man who'd gone for the bottles to come through, both his arms full.

'I got six.'

'Go and set them up,' Jimmy said.

The man placed them side by side on the street approximately twenty feet from where the two gun-fighters stood. Looking around, Laramie saw a stern-faced man standing off to the side of the crowd, a badge pinned to his chest. The sight of him reminded Laramie about the one still pinned to his own shirt.

'Are you ready, Davis?' Jimmy asked.

'You'll need someone to call it, kid. Just to make it fair.'

'I'll do it,' said the man who'd found the bottles, with more than a hint of exuberance. He took out his gun and pointed it in the air. 'Get yourselves ready.'

Laramie and Jimmy turned to face the bottles.

'Just one at a time, Davis.'

'I guess.'

'OK, then. Whenever you're ready, Rex,' said Jimmy.

Rex's gun roared and hands dove for gun butts. Jimmy's gun made a resounding crack and the bottle he'd fired at shattered. Laramie's did the same about a tenth of a heartbeat afterward.

The crowd cheered at the sight of it. The young gun had bested the Legend and they started to swarm about him.

'Back off,' cried Jimmy. 'We ain't done yet. Best of three, Davis?'

'Sure, kid. Why not?'

The crowd went back to their positions and Rex raised his gun into the air once more. The hammer fell and the weapon discharged. Again, hands flashed down for the same outcome.

The ensuing cheer from the crowd as it surged forward had Laramie turning away and starting to walk off. He caught sight of Ruby standing where he'd left her. She wasn't looking at him, however, but at the Colt in his hand. His left hand.

When Laramie drew level with her, she said in a low voice, 'Thank you, Laramie.'

He looked down at the Colt and holstered it, then shrugged.

'Maybe he should find something else to do before it's too late, Ruby.'

The look in her eyes said it all. 'It's already too late.'

CHAPTER 10

The blue roan snorted its disgust at having to come to a halt at the edge of the tree line. The vista before both horse and rider was a large meadow with a stream running through it. Ford had been out since early morning checking all the claims along the line he'd seen on the map.

Judging by their surrounding terrain, he was reasonably sure his assumption was right. They were situated along a vein of ore.

Eventually, he'd deviated away from his course and found the cabin. The first indication that the log structure was occupied was the faint smudge of smoke climbing into the sky.

'What do you think, horse? Should we go and have a look?'

The roan snorted again and moved its head up and down, trying to encourage its rider to go on. Ford was about to comply when the high-pitched whinny of horses drew his attention to the corral behind the dwelling.

81

There were four horses in the lodgepole pine construction. This set Ford to thinking. How many outlaws were there hitting the claims? He recalled being told by two different witnesses that they'd seen four. Could this be their hide-out?

Ford reached down and took the Winchester from the saddle scabbard. The weapon was chambered for a .45-.75 calibre bullet, which could stop an angry bear in its tracks. He laid it across his thighs and urged the roan forward from beneath the trees. Once out in the bright sunshine Ford thumbed back the Winchester's hammer and kept his eyes fixed on the cabin.

Easing the horse to a halt outside the cabin, he was rather surprised that no one had seen his approach.

'Hello, the cabin.'

A string of curses emanated from within and the door flew open. Four armed men tumbled outside led by a face Ford recognized. Spike Connors.

'What the hell you think you're doing sneaking up on a feller like that?' Connors growled.

'I wasn't sneaking.'

'What do you want, anyhow? You lost or something? Or maybe you're *law*?'

By the look in the man's eyes, Ford knew right off that the outlaw had recognized him. Then when he snarled the last word of his sentence, the deputy had all the warning he needed. The Winchester swept around, and the hammer dropped. Flame belched from the carbine's muzzle and Connors was blown back in a tangle of arms and legs. He grunted as the bullet ripped through his guts, tearing at everything it touched.

Ford switched his aim and killed the man who'd been standing next to the outlaw leader. A well-placed slug stopped his beating heart almost instantly.

Beneath the deputy marshal, the roan hadn't moved. It remained transfixed where it stood.

When the foresight centred on the chest of the third man, the outlaw had a change of heart. Instead of trying to shoot Ford he threw his arms in the air and shouted, 'Don't shoot!'

The fourth outlaw was of the same idea and followed suit, his face full of fear.

Ford said, 'All right, here's your chance to convince me not to shoot you. Was it you lot who hit the Claims?'

'Yes, sir.'

'Who's your boss?'

'Connors.'

'No. The one who set this up. Your other boss?'

The man hesitated, and then said, 'Carlton.'

Carlton sprawled in the dirt of the main street and immediately covered his head waiting for another blow to land. His white shirt was now covered with brown stains that matched the colour of the ground beneath him. Ford grabbed him by the collar and snarled, 'Get up, you son of a bitch.'

He dragged him to his feet by the collar and Carlton let out a yelp and staggered as the deputy started to drag him along the street to the jail.

The assayer stumbled and went down on one knee. Ford cursed at him and yanked hard on the shirt. Carlton's boots scratched at the earth as he tried to get purchase to regain his feet.

'Come on, damn you, get up.'

'What ... what are you doing? Somebody, help me! He's crazy.'

'Stop your hollering, Carlton. I have witnesses in jail who'll swear you were behind it all.'

Suddenly Ford was aware of a horse beside him. He looked up and saw the smiling face of Laramie looking down at him.

'You need a hand, Josh?' he asked.

'Nope.'

'Roy Willis said you should be about wrapped up. Guess he was right. He said . . .'

Ford stopped as though he'd run into a heavy plank wall. 'If he said this was damned easy, I'm apt to hire you to go shoot him.'

Laramie's smile broadened. 'I don't do that anymore, remember?'

'Yeah, well.'

'He said I should come find you. There's something that needs looking into that will need both of us.'

'Where?'

'Storm.'

CHAPTER 11

Two-Gun George Butler rode into Storm amid a hive of activity. There were at least a dozen men working at cleaning up the town to make it habitable for the expected influx over the next few days. Big Kev Riordan had been updated on the progress of Li Chin, and the wagon with its valuable payload would arrive in five more days. Closer to two weeks than the original week or so he'd told Brown.

Behind Butler came a wagon. Normally it wouldn't have drawn much attention, except for the fact that this one was filled with women. Four of them to be exact. Honey drove while Tina sat on the seat beside her. Cheyenne and Clara sat in the back. They all looked hot and bothered and in need of a good wash, but at least they had arrived at their destination.

Suddenly one of the men noticed them and immediately fell in behind the wagon. Steadily others joined him until nearly every man was following the lumbering conveyance.

'What the hell is going on here?' Big Kev roared when he saw the spectacle.

Honey drew the wagon to a halt and glanced behind her. She smiled. 'Hi, boys.'

They all surged forward and gathered around them like drowning men reaching a desert island. One of the men said, 'Well, howdy, missy.'

'You all look like the eager kind,' Honey responded.

'That's something we all are. Yes, ma'am.'

'I'll ask again, what the hell is going on?' Big Kev growled. Honey stared at him and smiled.

'We're your entertainment. You got somewhere we can set up?'

'The saloon should be open tomorrow. That will do.'

'Why, thank you, sugar.'

'And don't call me *sugar*. I'm Big Kev, and this is my town.'

'Yes, sir, sugar.'

The killer scowled at them.

'My name is Two-Gun George Butler,' the rider said. 'I'm here for the festivities.'

Big Kev smiled. 'Pleased to meet you, Butler. Find yourself a room at the hotel. I'll come and see you there.'

'Thank you kindly, sir.'

Honey watched as the gunfighter kept riding along the street. She wondered how many others were in town.

*

Ford and Laramie stared at Roy Willis as they discussed the Storm situation. The marshal said, 'It would appear that Big Kev Riordan had a son. Mean son of a bitch who beat a whore to death over in Carter's Bend. Red Rivers took exception to the fact and killed him.'

'Who is Big Kev?' Ford asked.

'A bad man from St Louis. Has a finger in a lot of pies. It appears he has put up ten thousand dollars as prize money for the gunman who can kill Rivers.'

'Invitation only by the looks of it,' Laramie said. 'I ran into one of them over in Bucheron. A kid by the name of – get this – Jimmy the Kid. He travels with a large entourage that includes his mother. I know her from my past.'

'Christ, no,' Ford mumbled.

'Oh, yeah. There's a new punk in town.'

'He must be good though, if he rated an invite to the party,' Willis said.

Laramie nodded. 'Don't get me wrong. He's good all right. Do we know of any others who were invited?'

'Word has it Scar Fletcher is on his way along with Gentleman Jim Brown. Two-Gun George Butler, too.'

'And Laramie Davis,' Laramie said. Willis nodded slowly.

'OK. You want in?'

'Yes, it'll get me into the town.'

'That leaves Red Rivers,' Ford said.

'I can't see him doing this willingly,' Laramie said. 'Not the Red I know.'

87

Willis sighed. 'So, we must assume that he's an unwilling participant.'

'Which means we'll have to free him and get him out somehow,' Ford stated. 'Once we have him located we can free him.'

'You'll need a diversion,' Willis pointed out.

Laramie said, 'A town full of gunfighters – shouldn't be hard to come up with something.'

Willis nodded. 'All right. Good luck. And stay alive. I don't fancy telling Bass that I got two of his best agents killed.'

Ford smiled. 'We'll use the utmost caution, Roy.'

'And you saying that, Josh, scares the hell out of me.'

By the time Scar Fletcher arrived in Storm, the town was jumping. Word had spread far and wide and the population of the ghost town, normally steady at zero, had exploded to four hundred. People were camped in rundown houses out in the back blocks, on the edge of town in tents and covered wagons. The spectacle had become more than Big Kev Riordan could ever have hoped for.

A young man approached Fletcher as he crossed the town limits.

'Hey, mister, are you Scar Fletcher?'

'Go away, kid.'

'You are, ain't you?'

Fletcher kept riding, rocking with the fluid motions of his horse. His passage took him past a man hanging blue and white bunting from the front of what looked to be an old dry-goods store. The man turned, saw the rider and almost fell from the ladder as he recognized him.

Scrambling down, he started to run along the boardwalk, almost tripping over a raised plank, warped with age. Scar watched him disappear into the saloon. By the time he reached it a small crowd had started to gather outside. At their head was a big man.

Fletcher turned his horse toward the hitch rail, where it stopped and stood patiently.

'If I'd have known I was going to draw a reception like this, I'd've worn something special,' he remarked.

'You Scar Fletcher?' Big Kev asked.

'I am. Who's asking?'

'Big Kev Riordan.'

Fletcher nodded. He indicated the bunting and said, 'Looks like you're going all out.'

'Nothing's too good for my boy,' Big Kev growled.

Fletcher frowned.

'Rivers killed my son,' Big Kev said. 'This is all about him.'

'I didn't ask,' Fletcher told him.

'Well, I'm telling.'

'OK. Where *is* the famous gun?'

'He's not here yet.'

Sparks flashed in the bounty hunter's eyes.

'If I've rode all this way—'

'Easy, Fletcher,' Big Kev said, trying to soothe the man's anger. 'He'll be here. Just make yourself at home. Find a place to stay and come for a drink. It's all on me.'

Just then Brown moved through the crowd, coming to stand near Big Kev. Fletcher's eyes flicked across to him. He nodded.

'Jim,' he said.

'Scar. Been a while.'

'Yep. You in on this too?'

'Sure am. So is George Butler.'

'Who else you invite, Riordan?' Fletcher asked.

'Does it matter?'

Fletcher nodded. 'Does to me. Feller in my business makes a lot of enemies.'

'Jimmy the Kid and Laramie Davis.'

'Now ain't that interesting? You invited the Legend himself.'

'They say he's good.'

'*Was* good. He's a little over the hill these days.'

'I guess we'll find out. If he gets his chance.'

'I guess we will,' Jim Brown said cryptically.

CHAPTER 12

The arrival of Jimmy the Kid and his entourage was as raucous an entry into town as was ever seen. And they swelled the population of the town by at least thirty men and women. From the moment they hit the edge of the town limits, their noise could be heard across the whole town. To announce their appearance, Jimmy had a man blow his bugle.

'Wake them up,' he said. 'Let them know that the real entertainment has arrived.'

Toward the rear of the crowd came Ruby, riding in a buggy. She looked tired and worried. Scared that her son, who was still a boy, was about to enter something that there was no coming back from.

'Blow it again!' Jimmy cried out.

The brassy tones resounded along the street, drawing those who were inside, out to watch the bawdy spectacle.

Jimmy had stopped at the outskirts so that he could climb from his horse and into a wagon bed where he now stood like a young red-headed god with one of Ruby's girls hanging off each arm.

The bugle was the fanfare to announce his presence. The presence of the kid who would be king.

Along the street in the saloon Brown and Fletcher looked at each other over the tops of playing cards when they heard the commotion. Behind them, people started to move toward the new batwings and filter out onto the boardwalk.

'What do you suppose that is?' Brown asked Fletcher, throwing some money into the pot. 'Raise you five.'

Fletcher studied the worn cards in his hand.

'Why don't you get some new cards, Jim? These are about all done in.'

'If I did that, how would I know which card is which?'

'Fold.' Fletcher snorted with disgust and threw his cards in the centre of the table. He stared at Brown and shook his head.

'What?'

'You could have mentioned that before you took me for twenty dollars,' he growled. Then Fletcher turned to the barkeep. 'Bring us a new pack of cards if you have one.'

'Yes, sir.'

Fletcher then turned back to Brown. 'You're a damned cheat, Jim.'

Brown smiled. 'It makes life interesting.'

The bugle trumpeted again and as Butler walked past their table he said, 'You all coming out for a look?'

92

Fletcher said, 'Might as well. All I'm doing here is losing.'

He rose from his seat and took his hat from the chair to his right. Brown looked up at him as though he was sorry to see him go. Then he too came to his feet. 'Might as well see what it's all about.'

They stepped out onto the crowded boardwalk and pushed their way through to the front of the crowd where they found Big Kev with a scowl on his face.

'What's going on?' Brown asked.

'A damned circus is what,' Big Kev growled.

'It is what you've made it be,' Fletcher pointed out.

'That's right, damn it! It's *my* circus. Not some upstart punk's. Look at the little shit.'

Fletcher could see all right. The kid in the wagon with a girl on each arm and a crowd following him like he was some kind of Messiah.

'I say,' Butler said, sounding nonplussed. 'He's only a boy. Probably not even old enough to drink.'

'*Quiet!*' Big Kev roared. 'What the hell is all this horse-crap shenanigans?'

'Hey there, pard,' Jimmy called out.

'Don't you call me, pard, you young upstart,' Big Kev seethed. 'Who are you?'

'I'm Jimmy the Kid.'

'You're a noisy little shit, is who you are,' Fletcher growled.

Jimmy's expression changed. His eyes grew hard, his voice icy. He let go of the two whores and eased them aside.

'Excuse me a minute, ladies, old Scarface here has taken issue with our festivities.'

'You need to show a bit of respect, kid,' Brown said. 'Especially for your betters.'

'If they're here I don't see them.'

All of a sudden it was so quiet you could have heard a fly fart. The challenge was out there and it was almost certain that one, if not all the gunfighters would take up the challenge.

It was Two-Gun George Butler who stepped forward.

'Uppity little bastard, aren't you? Well, I'm in for the dance.'

'Anytime you're ready, Miss Mary.'

'*Enough!*' Big Kev snarled at the top of his voice. 'You are not here to fight each other. You are here at my invitation. Anyone who kills another will be dealt with.'

'How do you propose to do that?' Fletcher asked.

Big Kev raised a hand in the air and the surrounding rooftops suddenly sprouted shooters with Winchesters, aimed and pointed down at the street.

'That's how I propose to do that.'

Jimmy smiled. 'OK, you win.'

Laughter sounded from the crowd, which had a ripple effect until everyone was chuckling. The tension was broken.

Big Kev said, 'All right, find yourselves somewhere to stay. We're still waiting on our guest of honor and one more gun.'

'Who's that,' asked Jimmy.

'Laramie Davis.'

*

Rivers was sure that the tumbleweed wagon was about to fall apart. A couple of days earlier the wheels had started to screech like banshees, turning on axles in desperate need of a coat of grease. The day after Jimmy and his entourage had arrived in Storm, the wagon had navigated the foothills and was now on the last leg of the journey into its destination.

The wagon forded a creek about a mile from town, its steel-rimmed wheels grinding their way across the rounded stones at the bottom of the waterway before the straining team dragged it free of the flow to the other side.

Li Chin moved his horse in beside the wagon.

'Not long now, Rivers,' he said. 'We will soon be at Storm and you will get to meet Mr Riordan.'

Sarcasm laced Rivers' voice, 'I can't wait.'

'I never asked,' Li Chin said. 'Why did you kill his son?'

'He deserved it.'

'We all knew that. I want to know why? The woman was a whore.'

'She was still a woman,' Rivers explained. 'She didn't deserve what he did to her.'

They moved further along the road, silence enveloping them. Rivers studied Li Chin for a moment then asked, 'Why do you work for him?'

'I came here with nothing and he offered me a job. I couldn't even speak English. But I worked hard at my job and learning to talk your language. Soon I was good at both.'

'So, you're a killer just like him.'

'If you put it that way.'

'There's the town,' the driver said. His name was Miller. Li Chin nodded.

'Make the most of today,' he said to Rivers, 'because tomorrow you may be dead.'

Not if I can help it, Rivers thought to himself.

Outside the saloon the wagon came to a halt and people swarmed up on it to get a look at the stone-cold killer named Red Rivers.

'He don't look like much,' one man said.

Another chimed in, 'I thought he'd be bigger.'

'Just goes to show,' said his friend. 'You can't believe all you hear.'

Two women pushed up to the bars. They wore low-cut gowns and more face-paint than should ever be worn. It made their faces look like pale china. One of them smiled at him, revealing blackened teeth that looked like they were all about to fall out. Then she said to her friend, 'He's quite handsome. Pity he's locked up, a roll in the hay with him I'd enjoy.'

Her friend's dry cackle sounded above the noise of the crowd. 'You'd roll in the hay with anyone.'

'Don't you think he's cute?'

Her friend raised her hand to her chest and ran a finger down her grime-smeared cleavage. 'Of course.'

'Clear off,' another female voice snarled at them and Rivers saw Honey push through the crowd behind the women. She had on a blue dress which accentuated the swell of her breasts. 'Get gone before I bury both your ugly heads into the street.'

With an indignant look, the two women pushed back through the crowd. Honey reached through the bars and Rivers scooted across to talk to her.

'What are you doing here?'

'I heard what was happening,' she said hurriedly. 'The girls and I came to see if we could help.'

Rivers shook his head. 'No. Leave it alone. I'll be fine.'

'We can help.'

'No—'

'All right. Get away from the wagon,' Big Kev barked from the boardwalk. 'Let me have a look at our guest of honour.'

The crowd parted and Honey slipped away. It was then that Rivers first saw the man who so desperately wanted him dead, walking down the steps. Big Kev stopped beside the wagon and stared at his prisoner. There was a range of emotions that flooded his face but then they settled down and the man smiled.

'You did well, Chin.'

'He never give us any trouble.'

'Good. I want him in top shape for when we start the festivities tomorrow.'

'I can see the resemblance now,' Rivers said. 'Your kid was an asshole like you.'

Anger flared in Big Kev's eyes at the mention of his dead son. He grasped the bars tightly with his hands until his knuckles turned white.

'You are going to get yours, murderer.'

'Not man enough to do it yourself, are you?' Rivers asked, goading the large man.

'Why have a dog and bark yourself?'

'Why indeed?'

'Get some rest, Rivers. Tomorrow will be a big day for you.' Big Kev was about to turn away when a voice said 'Where do I sign on for this shindig of yours?'

Every person, male and female, turned to see who was speaking. A murmur rippled through the crowd when they saw the man on the white horse. He was dressed in black and wore twin Colts around his waist. About his black low-crowned hat was a band made of silver conchos. His greasy hair hung down past his collar and an air of death seemed to emanate from him much the way it did from Scar Fletcher.

'Who are you?' asked Big Kev.

'Vince Polson, or Slick Vince as folks call me.'

'I don't seem to remember inviting you, Polson.'

'I don't recall getting one. But me and Rivers go way back. When I heard about what was going on, I thought I'd come and join in.'

Big Kev's reply was final. 'No.'

'Go on,' Rivers urged from inside his mobile cage. 'Why not have one more? Come on, Kev. What do you have to lose?'

'All right, Polson. You're in. Any trouble and my men will take care of you.'

'Me? Trouble? Never.'

PART 3

GUN THUNDER!

CHAPTER 13

The fire crackled and then popped, sending a small shower of sparks rising into the air; little orange dots that floated upward on the thermal. Ford stirred the fire some more with the stick in his hand.

'Horses are fine,' Laramie said as he walked out of the darkness and sat across from his fellow deputy marshal.

'We should sight Storm come mid-morning,' Ford said.

'We'll have a better picture then.'

'Do you know many of the fellers who'll be there?'

Laramie thought for a moment as he searched the recesses of his mind.

'I met the Kid – you know about him. Jim Brown I know from a couple of years back. Seen him in Wichita. George Butler I never met. Scar Fletcher, on the other hand, is another thing altogether. He's a pure killer. For him, it's about money. He's fast, but I'd say Red has him beat. Got them all beat if you ask me. Except for maybe Jimmy. That would be a close-run thing.'

'Remind me not to go against them any time soon.'

Laramie's face grew serious. 'Don't sell yourself short, Josh. I've seen you in action, remember? You're just as fast as any of them.'

'I don't want to be fast. I want to be alive.'

'Don't we all?'

'I'm going to turn in.'

'Yeah, me too. Big day tomorrow.'

'Well I guess the life has come back into the town,' Ford noted, looking at the bunting along the street. 'And all these folks seem mighty interested in you.'

'I guess that's the price of fame,' Laramie allowed. 'Keep an eye out.'

They rode up to the saloon, and as with the previous arrivals, the crowd gathered and moved in a wave with them. They dismounted and climbed the steps onto the boardwalk, boots clunking on the dry wood.

Laramie entered first, pushing the batwing doors open and stepping inside. Ford followed him and stood on his left. The room went silent and all eyes were drawn to the newcomers. Ford said, 'I always wanted to have a captive audience.'

'Looks like we got one,' Laramie said.

A chair scraped back on the wooden floor and a man came to his feet. Laramie recognized him instantly. It was Jim Brown. The gunfighter walked toward them.

'I do believe we have a *legend* amongst us,' Brown remarked.

Laramie held out his hand. 'Knock that shit off, Jim.' Brown took it.

'Always the humble one, Laramie. Who's your friend?'

'This is Josh,' was all Laramie offered.

Ford and the gunfighter shook. 'Pleased to meet you, Josh.'

Ford nodded. Brown's interest turned back to Laramie.

'I didn't think you'd be in for something like this.'

'Thought I'd come for a look.'

'Well then, I hope I get my chance before you. I can't see anyone getting a go after you.'

'Maybe he's slowed down some,' a new voice chimed in.

Eyes drifted to Jimmy who stood there with a large grin on his face like he'd just eaten the last piece of candy in the jar.

'Maybe I have, Kid.'

'Have some respect, young man,' Brown said. 'This here man has had more gunfights than you've had birthdays.'

'He wasn't that fast when I ran into him in Bucheron. I outdrew him on every occasion.'

Brown glanced at Laramie and gave him a questioning look. The deputy marshal nodded.

'It's true. Every time.'

'If that is true, what were you shooting at?'

'Bottles.'

102

Brown tried not to smile. 'I see. Dangerous, were they? Desperadoes?'

The room broke out into laughter. The Kid was learning a harsh lesson and Laramie wondered how he would take it. Jimmy said, 'It don't matter what we were shooting at. I still beat him.'

'What hand was he shooting with?' this came from Scar Fletcher.

'His left.'

'Uh huh.'

'What?'

Laramie glanced around the room and then he saw her. Ruby was sitting at a table on her own; that same expression of fear he'd seen on her face the last time.

'Laramie is right-handed, son. If you beat him and he was using his left hand, I'd say there was a reason.'

Jimmy's eyes flared. His burning gaze focused on Laramie, searing holes into him.

'Is that true?'

'I guess.'

'Why? Why'd you shoot left hand? Was it to make a fool of me?'

Laramie just shrugged.

'*Tell* me!'

'It's because he's had a bellyful of shooting young hotheads like you,' Ford snapped.

Jimmy smiled. If he couldn't get the Legend to bite, then maybe his friend would.

'You got something to say?'

'Seems to me, Kid, that Laramie would rather ride

a mile out of his way than draw on you. I have no such inclination. You're all mouth and deserve to be taken down a notch or two.'

'Oh dear,' Brown sneered. 'This one has teeth. Look out, Jimmy, I've a feeling that he bites.'

Jimmy got up from his table and walked away from it. 'Nothing I can't handle.'

Suddenly a drunk appeared beside Ford.

Staring at him through glazed eyes, he said, 'I know you.'

'Go away.'

'Yeah, I do,' the drunk slurred. He raised up a finger. 'You're him. You—'

It was almost too quick for the eye to see. Ford's hand blurred and the Peacemaker came up and crashed down on the drunk's head. He dropped like a pole-axed steer and went still. Brown chuckled.

'That'll do it.'

'I do declare,' a voice came from behind Laramie and Ford. 'Someone better have a good explanation for what I just saw.'

Standing there was Big Kev and two riflemen. Ford looked at him and said, 'Feller was crowding me. He learned better.'

'Who are you?'

'He's Josh,' Laramie cut in.

Annoyed, Big Kev's eyes focussed on the deputy marshal.

'Who are you, then?'

'Laramie Davis.'

CHAPTER 14

'All right. Now that you're all here, it's time to get down to business,' Big Kev's voice boomed around the saloon. 'You will each draw lots to see where you go in the line. The first one will go today. No sense in waiting. Then two more tomorrow, and the rest the next day. That's providing it gets that far.'

'I have a question,' Ford called from his table.

'What is it? And why are you asking questions? You ain't part of this.'

'What happens if none of them beat him?'

Jimmy snorted with disgust at the suggestion that anyone was better than him. Ford glared at him, but the kid looked away ignoring him.

'Then I keep my money,' Big Kev told him. 'But either way, Rivers doesn't leave here alive.'

It was at that moment that Ford had the mental image of the ancient Romans and their games which he'd heard about as a boy. Only Storm was the Colosseum, the gunfighters were the gladiators, and Big Kev was the emperor overseeing it all.

Ford and Laramie hadn't expected there to be a gunfight so soon after their arrival. The best they could hope for was that Rivers made it through the first one and that Laramie wasn't to be that man.

'Get me a pack of cards,' Big Kev snapped.

'I have one,' Jim Brown said.

'Not damn likely,' Fletcher protested. 'Get another deck.'

One was found, a new pack straight out of the box. Big Kev shuffled them and then spread them out flat on a table. 'You all take one. Highest card goes first. Then down the order that way. Everyone come up and pick a card.'

One by one, the gunfighters walked to the table and selected a card. Then they turned them over. Jim Brown smiled when he turned over the Ace of Spades, but that was quickly wiped from his face when Butler turned over the Ace of Diamonds. Jimmy drew the Jack of Hearts and Fletcher the Three of Clubs.

That left Laramie and Polson. The latter turned the Eight of Hearts while Laramie picked the Five of Spades.

'Wonderful, we're all done. The first to fight will be George Butler. You will be required at three this afternoon.'

'I'll be there.'

'Good. This should be fun.'

Laramie sat down at the table with Ford. He scooped up a bottle and poured himself a drink. He knocked it back and poured another. Ford stared at him and asked,'What's up?'

'I was hoping they wouldn't start until tomorrow.'

'Can Rivers take Butler?'

'I think so, but I was hoping to stop the deaths before they started.'

Ford said, 'There's ten thousand in the pot, Laramie. There's going to be killing no matter how you look at it.'

'Yeah. Let's hope it ain't us.'

With five minutes to go, Li Chin along with two guards went to the jail and opened the door of the cell so Rivers could come out.

The Chinaman looked at him and said, 'It's time.'

Rivers climbed up off the foul mattress and walked towards the door.

'Who's first?'

'Two-Gun George.'

Rivers sighed and with a hint of sadness in his voice said, 'I guess we all got to go someday.'

Once on the outside of the cell, his path was blocked by a guard who lifted a set of leg irons and said, 'These are for you.'

The gunfighter glanced at Li Chin. 'You worried I'll run away?'

Li Chin just smiled.

Once the leg irons were on Li Chin gave Rivers his own Colt. Rivers strapped the gunbelt on and checked the Colt for ammunition. It was empty.

'Am I supposed to throw rocks at him?'

Li Chin reached into his pocket and took out two

.45-calibre bullets for the Peacemaker.

'Big Kev said to give you only one, but I figure you may occasionally need that extra one.'

Opening the loading gate, Rivers slipped both rounds into the cylinder. Then he snapped it shut and placed the six-gun back into its holster.

'Are you ready?' Li Chin asked. The gunfighter stared at him.

'That would be a dumb question.'

They went outside and stood on the boardwalk. The sun was bright, and Rivers let his eyes adjust to the glare before he stepped down onto the street with a jingle of the leg irons' chain to accompany him.

Two-Gun George Butler stood no more than twenty feet away, waiting patiently. He called out to Rivers and said, 'Don't take this too personal, Rivers. It's just about the money.'

Red ignored him and looked about. It was a total circus. The bunting, the crowd; he was actually surprised not to see someone selling tickets to the show. He returned his gaze to Butler.

Big Kev stepped forward and climbed a stand specially made for him. He cleared his throat and shouted 'The time is here for the first battle. All you have to do, George Butler, is kill Rivers, and the money is yours. Simple, isn't it?'

Butler didn't like the fact that Big Kev made light of the fact that someone was about to die. After all, it could be him. He said, 'If it was easy, you could do it yourself.'

Big Kev glared at him.

From the boardwalk, Ford and Laramie watched on. They could feel the tension building in the crowd. Beside Ford stood Honey. The deputy marshal didn't know her name, but he'd seen her in the saloon. For some reason she kept staring at him. Now she was right there. She spoke to him out of the corner of her mouth.

'I need to talk to you after this.'

'Who are you?' Ford asked.

'Room six at the saloon,' she said, ignoring the question. 'I'll be waiting for you. Bring your friend if you need to.' She slipped back into the crowd.

'What was that about?' Laramie asked.

'I'm not sure.'

They turned their attention back to the proceedings. Big Kev had gone silent now to leave the combatants to their own devices.

Silence! Quiet and deafening at the same time. The two men stared at one another across the killing field, waiting for the other to make the first move, a kind of code.

'*Draw!*'

The high-pitched shout from the Kid pierced the air and triggered blurred reactions. Hands streaked toward gun butts. Fingers wrapped around them like an eagle's talons plucking a fish from a mountain stream. The weapons slid from holsters in a fluid motion, came up level, cocked and ready to fire.

Fingers caressed triggers and weapons belched, flame and smoke exploded from the barrels. Bullets, invisible to the naked eye, reached out across the seemingly short distance and only one found its mark.

Butler grunted under the impact of the slug from Rivers' Colt. He doubled over and took a step back. The expression on his face said it all when he looked up at his killer. Then the strength went out of his legs and his knees buckled. He fell to a kneeling position, his six-gun falling from his hand.

Finally, Two-Gun George Butler fell onto his side and didn't move, eyes wide, chest expanding until finally, it stopped as his heart ceased to beat.

Uproar burst from the crowd as they rejoiced in the death of one man, as well as the certainty of the spectacle continuing the following day. Rivers holstered the Colt and let his head slump forward.

'All right, lock him up!' Big Kev shouted. 'The next fight will be in the morning when Mr Brown will be up.'

Ford saw the look on his friend's face and when the gunfighter took a step forward, he said, 'Laramie. Leave it.'

'The punk's got to learn,' Laramie snapped and strode purposefully towards Jimmy.

It wasn't until the deputy marshal was almost on top of him that the kid realized that he was even there. He'd been too busy joking with his friends. By then it was too late. Jimmy's hand went for his gun, but Laramie's left hand clamped down on it in a grip that would almost crush rock. His right hand came up and around in a back-handed blow which stung the young gun's cheek. Ruby gasped in alarm at the sight of the deputy marshal's imposing form looming over her son.

For a moment there was actual fear in Jimmy's eyes and Laramie saw him for the kid that he was. But just as quickly as it appeared, it was gone. Laramie's harsh voice cut through the air like a knife. 'You shout like that again, you little shit, and you won't get to face Rivers. It'll be me standing twenty feet from you with a smoking Colt. Got it?'

Laramie released his grip on the kid's gun hand and turned away. Ford tensed and dropped his hand to his Peacemaker, expecting Jimmy to draw. But he didn't. Instead, he turned and stalked off through the crowd. When the deputy marshal drew close, Ford said, 'You'll need to keep an eye out from now on.'

'I'll be fine. He ain't a backshooter. He's too proud for that. When he comes after me, I'll see him coming.'

'You had to do it,' Ruby hissed at him as she appeared at their sides. 'The great Laramie Davis. Had to be a big man and humiliate him in front of everyone. In front of all his friends.'

'He's a boy playing in a man's world, Ruby. It's time someone showed him.'

'Did it have to be you? You know he won't let it go.'

'You'll have to convince him otherwise,' the deputy marshal told her. 'Because if he comes after me with a gun, this time I won't use my left hand.'

CHAPTER 15

'What did the whore want?' Laramie asked Ford as they entered the saloon.

'We're about to find out,' Ford said. 'Room six.'

As they crossed the floor towards the stairs Laramie looked around the room. He caught sight of Jimmy sitting alone at a table, brooding over what he hoped wasn't a glass of whiskey. They walked up the stairs and found room six halfway along the poorly-illuminated hallway. Ford knocked on the door and heard muffled voices from behind it. The doorknob rattled and the door swung open. Honey stood there and glanced at them both. She nodded and stepped aside. 'Come on in.'

Closing the door behind them, she walked over to join the others sitting on the bed. The room was small, cramped, dusty. More like an oversized box.

'What's this all about?' Ford asked.

Honey said, 'My name is Honey, these are Tina, Clara, and Cheyenne.'

'Ladies,' Laramie said by way of acknowledgment.

'You never answered my question,' Ford prompted.

'How about we start with the fact I know you're a deputy marshal,' Honey explained.

Ford's expression didn't alter. 'And?'

'We figure you're here for the same reason we are,' Tina supplied.

'Which is?'

'To help Red.'

Ford thought about lying but instead, he nodded. 'That's why we're here.'

'You too?' Honey asked Laramie.

'Yes.'

'Good. That *is* a relief.'

'What do you mean you're here to help Red anyway?' Ford asked.

'It was our friend that Johnny Riordan killed. He was the one that Red shot. He helped us out so we figure that we should do the same.'

'How?'

Honey's shoulders slumped. 'I don't know. But when I saw you, I knew that you were here for the same reason.'

'So, you came all this way without a plan? That's a crazy idea you all had,' Ford told them. 'Kind of reminds me of me.'

'The thing is,' Cheyenne said. 'If Honey can recognize you, then others will too. Like that man you dropped in the saloon.'

'But we took care of it,' Clara chimed in.

Laramie frowned. 'How?'

113

'He's tied up in the next room,' Cheyenne told them with a smile. 'Turns out he has a thing for red-heads.'

'There was always a chance that would happen,' Ford said to Laramie.

'Then we move tonight. I'll create a diversion and you go after Red at the jail.'

'That would be best.'

'Do you need any help?' Honey asked.

'No. You girls need to stay out of the way.'

The whore gave him an indignant look. 'Because we're women?'

'No,' Ford said with a shake of his head. 'Because this is dangerous.'

'You men are all the same.'

'No, we ain't. As you know. Be thankful for that.'

'What do you want, Ruby?' Jimmy snapped at his mother.

'I just wanted to see if you were OK.'

The Kid looked around the bar to see if anybody was watching. 'I'm fine.'

'Is that whiskey?'

'What if it is?'

Ruby sighed. 'That won't help, Jimmy.'

'No? Maybe shooting that son of a bitch will.'

She reached out and grabbed his arm. 'Don't you talk like that. You don't know what you're saying.'

'How about you tell me, *Ma*.'

'For a while now, I've been watching you practise with your gun. Every day drawing and shooting until you became fast. But that wasn't enough. I so hoped it would be, but no. Then you had your first gunfight and I prayed that would be it. But no, that wasn't good enough. You wanted – *had* – to be the best. And you can't stand it to think that someone might be better.'

'He humiliated me!' Jimmy seethed. 'Twice!'

'Be thankful he didn't kill you. Understand this, you cannot beat him. Not Laramie. You might have a chance against Rivers, but not him.'

'You have a lot of faith in me, Ma.'

'I know what he's like. I've seen him kill men quicker than you can blink. Don't go up against him.'

Jimmy studied her face for a moment and then nodded.

'All right, Ma. I'll let it go. Just this once.'

Ruby nodded. Happy that she might just have gotten through to her son.

A knock at the door brought both men to their feet. Ford walked to the door while Laramie stepped to the side with his Colt in his hand. With a turn of the handle, the door swung open and both men saw Jimmy standing there.

'What do you want?' Ford asked unpleasantly.

'I came to see Laramie.'

Ford looked at his friend and Laramie nodded. 'Come on in, kid.'

Ford closed the door behind him, and Laramie dropped the Colt into its holster. 'What is it, Jimmy?'

'I came to apologize about before.'

115

Laramie studied him. 'All right, kid, apology accepted. How's your ma doing?'

He shrugged.

'Why are you here, Jimmy?'

'Same as you.'

'I doubt that.'

'You're here for the money, ain't you?'

'Yeah, Jimmy. Sure. Go back and see to Ruby. Thanks for stopping by.'

Jimmy looked at him funny and then left. Ford looked at Laramie and said, 'What do you make of that?'

'Not sure. Besides, we don't have the time to worry about it.'

Ford said, 'Have you figured out a diversion for tonight?'

'You saw Polson?'

'Yeah.'

'He's my diversion.'

Nodding, Ford said, 'Couldn't happen to a nicer person. What are we going to do once we get Rivers out, though?'

'The way I figure it we've got two choices. We can get the hell out of town or go after Riordan.'

'I'm going after Riordan. Feller like him deserves a bullet.'

'I figured you would. The real question is, once everything is up in the air, which way will the remaining guns land?'

'You know them. Which ones are the most likely to still go after the money?'

116

'All of them.'

'But if we get rid of Riordan before it all goes to hell, then they'll have no one to pay them.'

'Sounds like a plan, but there'll still be his men. Especially the Chinese feller. I'm not sure how he'll react.'

'I guess we'll find out.'

'I guess we will,' Laramie said.

CHAPTER 16

Sundown came quickly and the darkness was broken by a silvery glow from a large moon perched above the distant hills to the east. With it came a chill, crisp night air which pricked the skin like fine needles. Ford slipped along behind the buildings, heading towards the rear of the jail. He figured Laramie would be in the saloon about now and ready to start something with Polson.

When Ford reached his destination he stopped outside the barred window and listened intently. When it seemed that all was quiet, he whispered, 'Red? Red Rivers?'

The deputy waited. Nothing happened.

'Red Rivers?'

'Who's there?' Rivers' harsh whisper came back.

'The name's Josh Ford. I'm a deputy marshal. I'm here with Laramie Davis. We're going to get you out.'

'How are you going to manage that?' Rivers asked.

'You leave that up to us. How many guards are there?'

'Two.'

'OK. I'll be there shortly.'

Ford made his way around the building and toward the front of the jail. Once there he remained in the shadows, waiting for Laramie to start his part.

It was a cold hard gun barrel pressed against the back of his neck that put everything on hold. It seemed to burrow into his skin and a voice asked, 'What are you doing around here?' It was Li Chin.

'Just out getting some air,' Ford said lamely.

'Really?'

'Yeah.'

The deputy felt his Colt leave its holster and Chin said, 'Inside the jail.'

Ford walked around and up the steps. He went in through the door and the two guards' jaws dropped when they saw him and Li Chin.

'What's going on, Li Chin?' a thin man asked.

'He was outside. Check his pockets.'

The second of the guards, thickset, early thirties, beard, stepped forward and checked all his pockets and found nothing except for some money. After he'd finished, he stepped back and frowned. Then he checked Ford's coat again. That was when he found the knife-slit on the inside. He reached in and took out the marshal's badge.

'Well, well, what do we have here?'

Ford looked at him with a hard gaze.

'I'll be getting that back,' he said.

Laramie sat, watching and waiting. It wasn't in his

nature to go out of his way to kill a man, but for Polson, he was willing to make an exception.

Polson was at the bar by himself drinking from a bottle. Laramie was about to stand up and start the ball rolling when the batwings opened, and Ford walked in. But he wasn't alone. Standing behind him was a Chinese man pressing a gun into the lawman's spine.

'What's damn well going on here?' Big Kev growled.

'It seems our friend here is a deputy marshal.'

Big Kev's eyes sought out Laramie. When he found him, he said, 'Explain yourself.'

'About what?'

'About why you brought this lawman here with you?'

Laramie looked at Ford. 'It's simple. I didn't know he was one. We met a few days before we got here. Travelling in the right direction and rode together.'

'Likely story for a lawman,' Polson snarled.

Laramie let his eyes grow flinty. 'Are you calling me a liar?'

'If the shoe fits.'

Laramie's hand dropped to his right-side Colt in a threatening gesture.

'Call it, Polson.'

'Be glad to.'

'Hold it!' Big Kev snapped. His gaze turned back to Ford. 'Who are you? Who are you, *really*?'

'Name's Josh Ford.'

The name brought forth a murmur from the

crowd. Many of them had heard of the marshal and his exploits. Even Big Kev.

'Looks like we have a famous person with us. What were you up to? Trying to get Rivers free?'

'What if I was?'

'Well, I guess it don't matter much anyhow. However, the question remains, what to do with you?'

'I have an idea,' Polson said with a mirthless smile.

'No,' Brown snapped. 'I didn't come here to be part of killing a lawman.'

'I'll do it,' Laramie said.

'What?' Big Kev snapped.

'I said, I'll do it. He tricked me and came here with me. So, I'll do it.'

The man from St Louis thought long and hard about it before he said, 'No.'

'Why not? You're looking for a chance to trust me. Let me prove it.'

Ford's blood ran cold. He knew Laramie was up to something, but not knowing what, did nothing to ease his mind.

'All right—'

And Laramie shot Ford.

CHAPTER 17

'Touch him and I'll kill you next!' Laramie snapped.

The man who'd taken a step forward, froze, looked and saw the Colt in Laramie's hand pointing at him. 'I – I was just—'

'You were just going to back off. I killed him, I'll get rid of the body. First lawman I ever shot. Can't say I'm particularly proud of it. Jim, give me a hand.'

Brown hesitated and stepped forward. 'All right, Laramie.'

'Wait,' Big Kev ordered.

'What for?' Laramie asked.

'I just wanted to say I'll still be watching you, Davis. Just because you shot him, doesn't mean I trust you.'

'I don't give two shits whether you do or don't,' Laramie snarled. 'If you want to continue this, then I'm ready right now.'

The guards with Big Kev came on edge, knuckles whitening as their grips tightened on their weapons.

'I'll stand with Laramie,' said Jimmy as he came to his feet.

'That won't be necessary,' Big Kev snapped. 'Get the damned body out of here. Out of town even. I don't want it stinking the place up.'

The deputy marshal housed his Colt and walked over to where Ford lay. Bending down, he waited for Brown who did the same and they lifted Ford, leaving behind a small pool of blood on the floor.

Once they had him outside, they walked around the corner of the saloon and into the alley. About halfway along, Brown said, 'Now?'

'Yeah. Now.'

They dropped Ford without ceremony to the hard-packed earth of the alley.

'Damn it,' he cursed out loud. 'You shot me.'

'Isn't he meant to be dead?' Brown asked.

'Yeah.'

'I don't know what the hell is going on, but—'

'Jim, I ain't never killed a lawman before and I ain't about to start now. Not for that son of a bitch.'

'OK.'

Laramie leaned down and said harshly, 'You get the hell out of town and don't look back. If I ever see you again, I *will* kill you.'

'Sure. OK,' Ford babbled. 'I'll get my horse and things and be gone.'

'Just don't get seen.'

Ford climbed to his feet and pressed his hand to his side. Pain shot through him and he gasped. He realized that for Laramie's ruse to work he needed blood, but still couldn't believe that his friend had actually shot him. Turning, he started to walk along the alley. 'Don't forget what I said.'

'I won't.'

'How could you?' Honey gasped desperately in the privacy of her room. 'You killed your friend.'

'Easy, woman, I only clipped him. He's still alive and the only ones who know are you, me, Brown and Ford. I'd like to keep it that way until we can work out what to do next.'

'Oh, thank God! I thought you'd killed him for sure.'

'Hopefully so do they. I had to make him bleed to make it look good. However, if they'd got a closer look, they would have found out otherwise. That was why I wouldn't let them touch him.'

'What about Brown?'

'He won't say anything. He didn't like the idea of killing Josh from the start.'

'OK. What's next?'

'I need to get a message to Red. Tell him to sit tight. Who takes him his food?'

'I don't think anyone does.'

'Good. Then you take him food tonight. Put something together and take it over.'

'But what if they won't let me?'

'Do your best. That's all you can do.'

Honey nodded. 'OK. I'll try.'

Rivers had been waiting for Josh for over an hour. In that time, he'd heard the shot and then the guards talking about the dead deputy marshal. That was when he realized that getting out of the mess he was in was once again up to him.

Something made him frown. Voices in the other room. He thought one was a woman's. He listened harder and heard, 'We were told not to give him food.'

'Well, your boss changed his mind.'

'He ain't said nothing to us.'

'Would you like to go and ask him? I'm sure he's a man who loves his orders being questioned.'

There was a brief silence followed by, 'OK. Make it quick. I'll need to search you first.'

'I'm sure you'll enjoy that,' said the woman, her voice laced with sarcasm.

Moments later the door opened, and Honey walked through holding a covered plate of food in her hands. Rivers came off his makeshift cot and crossed to the bars. Honey turned to face the man who'd let her in. 'How am I meant to get the food into him?'

'Your problem,' he said and closed the door. Honey turned and uncovered the plate. 'Before you say anything, just listen and eat.'

Rivers took the fork and started feeding himself while Honey held the plate.

'There's people in town who are working on getting you out of here.' Honey started to explain the plan. 'But you'll have to get through another day. Laramie will come for you tomorrow night.'

'What happened to that other feller? Said he was a marshal?'

125

'Don't worry about him.'

'I heard them say he was dead.'

'Just be ready,' Honey said. 'And stay alive.'

'Do you know who I'm fighting tomorrow? They won't tell me.'

'Brown and the Kid.'

Rivers nodded.

'Just remember they're trying to kill you for the money. They'll have no hesitation about doing it.'

Rivers' expression changed. 'I thought I told you to stay out of this, anyway?'

'I recall something like that.'

He stared into her eyes and said, 'I'm kind of glad you didn't.'

She touched his hand. 'It's the least we could do.'

The gunfighter finished off his food and placed the fork back on the plate.

'Thank you. That was mighty fine. You'll make someone a great wife someday.'

Honey blushed. No one had ever said anything remotely like that to her before.

'I'll see you in the morning. I'll bring you breakfast.'

'Condemned man's last meal?' he asked with a chuckle.

'Don't you say that!' she said fiercely. 'Don't even think it.'

'OK. I'll see you then.'

She let her hand linger for a moment longer and then let it fall. The door opened and the guard entered.

'You all done yet.'

'Yes,' Honey told him.

'Then you'll have to leave.'

One last glance at Rivers and she turned and left.

Ford hissed at the pain that shot through him as Cheyenne dabbed at his raw wound with a wet cloth. She looked at him in the orange glow of the small fire and said, 'Don't be a baby. I heard you were a big tough marshal who always gets his man.'

'Whoever told you that lied,' Ford growled. 'I like my blood to stay right where it is. I still can't believe Laramie damned well shot me.'

'He saved your life by doing it.'

'I'm not going to argue there.'

'Is there a Mrs Ford?' Cheyenne asked coyly, taking him by surprise.

Suddenly he was aware of her proximity. The red hair, green eyes, low-cut bodice of her dress, the touch of her fingers on his skin as she helped him remove his shirt. He shook his head. 'No.'

Cheyenne stared at him, studying his face.

'What?' he asked.

'Just looking. You're a handsome man, Josh Ford.'

'I wouldn't know.'

'Take it from me,' she said.

The lonesome howl of a wolf sounded throughout the foothills. Ford cleared his throat and said, 'Are you sure they won't miss you?'

'As long as I'm back by morning I'll be fine. Tina is telling everyone I'm not well.'

'No one saw you follow me out of town?'

'I grew up out West. My pa was a hunter who never had any sons. I can cowboy with the best of them. Are you trying to get rid of me after everything I've done for you?'

'Ahh, no.'

'Good.'

Cheyenne started to bandage him around his torso. The light touch of her breath on his skin every time she leaned in to wrap another layer sent small shocks through Ford. He turned his head and looked at her and she, in turn, looked at him. After a moment that seemed to go on forever, Ford gave in to the urge and kissed her.

When he drew back, the expression on her face almost brought forth an apology from him for being so forward. After all, they'd known each other a whole day. Maybe a little longer. But before he could utter a word Cheyenne said, 'Don't speak.'

Then she leaned in and they kissed again.

CHAPTER 18

Laramie stood with the rest of the crowd and waited for the duellists to appear. Beside him, wearing a red dress, was Honey.

'I don't know what your friend did to Cheyenne last night but she's full of smiles this morning.'

The deputy marshal stared at her. 'What are you on about?'

'She followed him out of town last night and doctored his wound. She's mighty handy like that. Anyway, ever since she's been back, she's been all moon-eyed and smiling.'

'She followed him out of town?' Laramie asked urgently.

'Sure did.'

'Christ, I hope she wasn't seen.'

'Don't worry about her. I swear she's part Indian.'

Nodding, Laramie asked, 'How was Red this morning?'

'OK, I guess.'

'Are you going to take him more food at noon?'

Honey paused. 'I hadn't really thought about it.'

'I need you to take him some food and another little package.'

'The guards search me, you know that?'

'I do. But I figure a woman with your skills can get around that.'

'God, I'm glad you're confident.'

'Meet me in your room after we've finished here.'

The sound of heeled boots clunking on the board-walk heralded the approach of Gentleman Jim. He stood beside the deputy marshal, took a deep breath, and said, 'It's a good day for it, Laramie. Smell that mountain air.'

'You don't have to do this, Jim,' Laramie said to him. Brown looked at him and smiled.

'If I can get that money, Laramie, then I'll be set. I can hang up my gun and do something else.'

'He's just using us all, Jim,' Laramie pointed out. 'You know that. We could all die out here in this damned place and he'll just use his men to finish the job. It's the spectacle he cares about. Revenge. He don't give a damn about us.'

Brown smiled at Laramie. 'It's what we do.'

Laramie cursed as Brown stepped down from the boardwalk. The crowd started to cheer and without hesitation, Jim Brown bowed.

'He's going to die, isn't he?' Honey asked.

'Yes,' the deputy marshal said. 'He's not fast enough.'

'Is there anyone amongst you who is?'

'Probably two men that I know of may match Red

for speed,' Laramie told her as the cheering carried on in the background.

'Who?'

'I'm one and Ford is the other.'

Realization hit Honey. 'That means Jimmy hasn't got a hope either.'

'That's right.'

'That poor woman.'

Meanwhile out on the street, Gentleman Jim Brown played up to the crowd as though it was his last performance.

When Rivers appeared, the crowd began to boo and throw insults his way. Upon reaching the centre of the street he stopped and turned to face Brown.

'You all know the rules,' Big Kev said.

No sooner had the words escaped his mouth than Rivers drew and fired. No warning, no wasting time. One moment Brown was alive, the next he was on his back in the middle of the street.

The crowd went wild and started to surge forward. The gunfighter stopped them, however, by pointing the smoking Colt in his fist towards them. They stopped as one. Though they had no clue that he still had one bullet left, not one of them wanted to risk being the person he fired at.

Laramie watched as Rivers started back towards the jail. Honey said, 'He never gave him a chance.'

'He couldn't afford to,' Laramie allowed.

'It was so cold.'

'This whole thing is cold,' Laramie growled. 'I do know one thing, though. This stops today.'

The sound of the coffin lid being nailed onto Jim Brown's pine box echoed along the main street. Laramie waited until it had stopped before going inside the saloon and starting up the stairs. He'd made it halfway when he heard a voice say, 'Jim Brown was too damned old and slow. Pure and simple.'

Laramie stopped and turned on the stairs. He looked through the gathered crowd to find the source of the voice and then saw him. Polson!

All his pent-up anger at the situation boiled to the surface and, instead of continuing his previous course up to the room, Laramie walked down the stairs. On hitting the floor-boards he turned and made a beeline toward the gunman.

By the time Polson saw Laramie, it was too late. He grabbed for his gun just as a hard, right fist crashed against his jaw. The gun fell from his grasp as he staggered along the bar. Laramie closed the distance with purposeful strides and hit him again. This time the gunman went down.

Laramie bent over him, reached down, and took the other six-gun from its holster. Then he straightened and snarled, 'Get up!'

Polson started to come to his feet. Halfway there, Laramie grabbed his collar and dragged him the rest of the way, then swung another blow, but Polson blocked it then fired one of his own back.

Laramie rocked on his heels from the stinging

blow, shook his head and then circled to his left to get away from the bar. Once in position, he charged the killer. But Polson was ready and he raised his right foot and drove it forward, stopping Laramie in his tracks and knocking the wind from his lungs.

The deputy marshal doubled over, sucking in great gulps of air. Polson lumbered over to him and brought a double-fisted blow down upon Laramie's back, driving him to his knees. Next, the killer tried to kick the deputy marshal in the head, but Laramie's reflexes were quicker than the killer's and he grabbed the man's boot and twisted savagely.

With a yelp, Polson fell to the floor and Laramie staggered back to catch his breath. The killer came to his feet and charged at the deputy marshal. Laramie hit him as he came; a solid blow which sounded like someone splitting wood with an axe. It didn't stop Polson however, and his shoulder crashed into the deputy's midriff.

With shouts of encouragement and frustration from the crowd, the pair hurtled onto a table with a splintering crash. Laramie could taste blood in his mouth as he fought to roll Polson from atop him.

'I'm going to kill you, you bastard,' Polson snarled.

Laramie brought his left fist crashing around twice. The first blow seemed to have no effect. The second loosened the man's grip and allowed Laramie to shove him away.

They staggered to their feet once more and stood toe-to-toe, trading blows. Finally, Laramie slipped a straight right through the killer's defences which split Polson's lips and busted his nose. The contact stunned him, and he lurched back against the bar.

The deputy closed in and hit him three more times. Polson's head rocked back with each blow, but the bar held him up even though his legs were getting weak. Laramie hit him twice more and it was over. The killer slid down the bar to the floor and stayed there.

Blowing hard, Laramie looked about the room. All eyes were on him, but not one person made a sound. He snorted and turned towards the stairs. Halfway up them he lifted his gaze and saw Honey standing at the top. As he stomped past her, she asked, 'Do you feel better?' He glared at her.

'No, I don't.'

While Honey cleaned up Laramie's cuts and scratches he outlined what he wanted done.

'I'll give you extra bullets to give to Red. Tell him to go ahead with the gunfight and be ready for what comes next.'

'OK. I can do that,' Honey said. The deputy glanced at Cheyenne.

'I heard you followed Ford out of town last night. How is he?'

She shrugged. 'OK, I guess. I cleaned up his wound for him. He's not overly happy with you shooting him, though.'

'Do you think you can find him again?'

'Sure.'

'Good. Head back out there and tell him to be in position by the time this afternoon's gunfight takes place. Tell him, somewhere high. On top of the old dry-goods store.'

Cheyenne nodded. 'I'll leave now.'

'And no distractions.'

Cheyenne turned the colour of her hair and gave him an embarrassed smile. 'I'll try.'

She slipped out the door and Clara asked, 'What about us?' Laramie nodded.

'Can you go and get Jimmy? Bring him back here?'

'Yes.'

'Do it.'

'What about me?' Tina asked.

'Can you shoot?' Clara asked. Tina nodded eagerly.

'Then find yourself a gun. You'll need it.'

PART 4

RAINING LEAD!

CHAPTER 19

Clara returned ten minutes later with Jimmy and Ruby in tow. Laramie frowned at the older woman.

'If you think I was letting him come up here to see you on his own you were sadly mistaken.'

'I already told you, Ruby. Me and Laramie are all good. Right?'

'I told you not to call me that,' Ruby snapped nervously.

'He's fine, Ruby.' Laramie tried to reassure her.

'See, I told you.'

The deputy stared at him. Although Jimmy played life and death in a man's world, he was still a kid. He said, 'Jimmy, I want you to back out from the gunfight this afternoon.'

All kinds of emotions dashed across the kid's face; the last one, however, was the one which stuck. Anger. He opened his mouth to snarl a rebuke when his mother cut him off.

'Before you say anything, Jimmy, how about you listen. I've a feeling that there is more to this than meets the eye.'

He nodded. 'I'm listening.'

'Your mother is right,' Laramie said. 'First off, you can't beat Red on the draw. And before you ask why – or any such thing – I think deep down you know that yourself. All that will happen is you'll wind up dead and you'll destroy your mother. Second, I need your help. I'm not a gunfighter anymore, I'm a deputy marshal. The same as Ford.'

Ruby gasped.

'And you still shot him,' Jimmy snapped skeptically.

'I did. But he's still alive.'

'What?'

'I don't have time to explain. When the gunfight starts this afternoon, things are going to happen. We aim to free Red and put an end to all this. I'm giving you a chance to walk away now or to help us. I sure could use a good extra gun.'

'I'm listening.'

'As soon as the shooting starts, Red will have a full chamber and Ford will be in position on the old dry-goods store roof. We could use your gun to even out the odds. What do you say?'

'OK, I'm in.'

'Fine. Tell Big Kev you want out. That'll bump Polson up the list. You clear with everything?'

'Sure, Laramie. I got it.'

'Good, I'll see you then.'

The door into the cell room opened and Honey was

shown through with Rivers' lunch. He walked across to the rusted bars and rubbed his hands down his pants. 'Steak and beans?' he asked with a wry smile. Honey shook her head. 'You should do that more often.'

'What's that?'

'Smile. It looks good on you.'

'Ain't had much to smile about lately,' he said.

'No.'

Honey placed the food on the floor and started to undo the top of her dress. Soon her corset and the tops of her breasts were exposed. Rivers' jaw dropped.

'What are you doing?'

She smiled at him. 'Don't go getting all excited. I've got something here for you from Laramie.'

Honey reached into her top and took out four bullets for the gunfighter's Colt.

'He said you'll need these.'

Rivers took them and stuffed them away in his pocket. 'I'm not sure what good they'll be, but I guess six shots are better than two.'

'They will be. Laramie said to tell you that it will happen today. This afternoon. He said all you have to do is keep shooting. There will be others in place to help out.'

'Just keep shooting?'

'Yes.'

'At what?'

'Anything that shoots back. His words, not mine.'

'All right; tell him thanks.'

'Shall we get you eating now?'

'Sure. Why not?'

Scar Fletcher raised the money in the pot by ten dollars and called. The man across from him smiled. He lay down his cards and said, 'Three Kings.'

Fletcher nodded and started to put down his cards.

'Uh huh, not bad. I got me three fours. But then the two Queens keep them company.'

The smile disappeared from the round face and was replaced by an expression one might find on a kid in a candy store who was told he couldn't have any.

'Shit.'

The bounty hunter raked the money towards himself and put it in a pile in front.

'Another hand?'

The man shook his head. 'No. I'm done.'

'Pity.'

'Not for you,' he said and got up from the table.

Fletcher sat there by himself and started to count his money. Suddenly he had a feeling that someone was watching, and he looked up. Seeing who it was he said, 'What do you want?'

CHAPTER 20

Ford was still where he'd been the previous evening when Cheyenne found him. He was behind a small clump of rocks large enough to block out any sight of the camp but close enough for Ford to see the town. The blue roan was further back in the trees.

It was the sound of a twig snapping that made him aware that someone had managed to sneak that close to his camp. He reached for the Winchester and winced as his wound pulled. He grabbed the carbine and tried to quietly thumb back the hammer.

'Josh, are you there?'

He relaxed; it was Cheyenne. He rose and walked around the rocks.

'I'm here.'

'Thank God! I was hoping you hadn't moved.'

He let down the hammer. 'What's up?'

'Laramie sent me here. He said for you to slip into town before the gunfight this afternoon. And to get up high. He said the old dry-goods store would be a good place.'

Ford nodded as they slipped back behind the rocks.

'Did he say what he has in mind?'

'Not really. I guess you'll find out when the shooting starts.'

Ford moved close to Cheyenne and slipped his left arm around her waist. He looked into her eyes and leaned in to kiss her. Cheyenne pushed him away.

'Hold it right there. I'm under strict orders to give you no distractions.'

Raising his eyebrows, the deputy asked, 'Laramie?'

'Yes.'

'He would take all the fun out of the situation,' Ford growled.

'He's right. Besides, I've been thinking. What happens after all this is over? You go back to whatever it is that you do, and I go back to whoring?'

Ford studied her face. For some reason, after the night before, he found himself constantly thinking about her. Her hair, her eyes, the way she felt. She was slim, kind, gentle. Way too good for her chosen profession. Not that most of them made the choice to sell themselves to men. It was often due to unfortunate circumstances that women were forced into it.

'What if—' he stopped.

'What if what?'

'What if I took you with me?'

Cheyenne looked at him strangely. 'Why would you do that?'

Don't stop now, Ford told himself. 'I have enough money saved to buy a small place I've had my eye on

142

for a while now. It ain't much but—'

'Good Lord, are you asking me to marry you?'

Ford's eyes widened. 'No! No, I ain't. I'm asking you to . . . ah hell, I don't know what I'm saying. Forget it.'

'OK.'

'Good. I don't—'

'OK, I'll come with you.'

The deputy almost fell over. 'You will?'

'Yes.'

'There's something you need to understand. I'm a deputy marshal.'

'I know that.'

Ford looked embarrassed as he stumbled over his words again.

'No, I mean that's what I do. I go away for a month or two at a time. You'd be on your own, but I would provide for you while I'm gone. You'd want for nothing. And like I said, I'm not asking you to marry me . . . just yet.'

'I know,' Cheyenne said with a nod. 'And I'm not expecting you to. We don't even really know each other yet. But that will come with time and the only way to do that is for me to come with you.'

'Are you sure?'

'Yes.'

He smiled and opened his mouth to say something else when from back in the trees he heard the roan give a warning snort. Ford reached out and touched Cheyenne's arm in a cautioning gesture. Her eyes immediately told him she understood.

Ford still held the Winchester in his right hand. He whirled and managed to bring it halfway up before he saw Big Kev's man, Li Chin, with his own weapon pointed at him.

'This is interesting,' he said, confused. 'For a dead man, you look rather well.'

Ford shrugged. 'What can I say? I look good as a ghost.'

'It makes me think that your friend is not who he seems to be. If you are a marshal, then he might be one too. Am I correct?'

Cheyenne edged to the side, out of the line of fire. Li Chin spotted her.

'You should be more careful, when you are going somewhere, that you're not followed.'

She cursed under her breath and took another step.

'Where are you going?' Li Chin asked.

'Me? I figure to get out of the way just in case you decide to pull the trigger on that thing. I'd hate to get hurt, especially when that thing in your fist blows up. Especially with that lump of dirt blocking the barrel.'

The comment was designed to distract the Chinese man. By rights it should never have worked, for they both figured Li Chin was smarter than that. But he wasn't and he glanced down at the barrel. It was all the time needed by Ford to bring the Winchester into play. He swung it up and around and thumbed back the hammer.

Li Chin realized his stupidity too late. He tried to

recover and bring the six-gun back into line with Ford. But the deputy had the advantage and the Winchester roared in his hands. The slug punched into the Chinese man's chest, tossing him back like driftwood on a wave. His arms flailed wildly as he tried to keep his balance. He lost his grip on his gun and sat down, hard.

Bewildered, Li Chin looked down at the fast-spreading patch of red on his shirt. He glanced up at Ford and opened his mouth to speak. All that came forth was a torrent of blood that spilled down his chin and onto his chest.

Then he slumped further forward and died.

'Damn it!' Ford swore. 'Cheyenne, keep a watch to see if anyone has heard.'

Still shocked at the violence she'd just witnessed, she hesitated.

'Cheyenne!' Ford snapped.

Her eyes never left the corpse. 'Yes?'

'Keep watch.'

'OK.'

He followed her with his eyes as she moved over and checked the body. The Chinese man had been armed with a Colt .45, so the deputy took it as a replacement for his own. He'd look for his Peacemaker once this was all over.

Ford dragged the body into the trees and hid it. Then he went back to Cheyenne. 'Anything?'

'No. It looks fine.'

'Good. Head back to the town and tell Laramie I'll be ready when he is.'

Cheyenne kissed him before she left and said, 'You stay alive, Josh Ford. I've a feeling you're a good man.'

CHAPTER 21

Laramie came down the stairs and headed for the bar. He caught sight of Jimmy sitting at his usual table and the kid nodded. Once the gunfighter reached the bar he said to the barkeep, 'I'll have a whiskey.'

While Laramie waited, the barkeep returned with a glass and bottle, filled it and asked, 'You want me to leave it?'

The gunfighter shook his head.

'Just one will do.'

Knocking the drink back, he turned and walked toward the batwings. It was time to get it done. Whether they lived or died depended on what happened next.

Outside, the crowd had gathered and Big Kev's men had a more obvious presence. That did not bode well for a start. But time would tell. All he had to do was wait.

'Out,' snapped the guard as the door swung open with a screech.

Rivers stepped through the opening and took the weapon and gun belt that were offered to him. He strapped the belt on and then checked the loads in the gun.

One of the guards stepped forward with his hand out. Rivers looked at him.

'What?'

'Hand them over.'

'Hand what over?'

'Don't play dumb, Rivers,' he said, indicating over his shoulder. 'If you try something Mort will cut you in half with the scattergun.'

Rivers reached into his pocket and took the bullets out. He held his hand open and the guard plucked them from his palm.

'Right, let's go.'

They left the jail and walked out onto the street. This time the guards escorted Rivers to the centre of the dusty thoroughfare where they remained on either side of him. Then Jimmy appeared with Big Kev. The man drew in a deep breath and called out at the top of his voice, 'Laramie Davis?'

Nothing happened.

'United States Deputy Marshal Laramie Davis!'

Rivers saw movement on the boardwalk and Laramie appeared.

'I'm here, Riordan,' he said.

Men with rifles suddenly appeared from alley mouths and on the balconies of the hotel and saloon. All had their weapons concentrated on the street. This was not good.

*

'Just stand up nice and slow, Marshal,' the voice behind Ford said. 'Nice and slow.'

Ford grimaced and mentally chided himself for being so careless. He'd been watching the happenings below, and now, with the man creeping up on him, the deputy knew that they had been betrayed.

Ford stood slowly as ordered. Now, from the street below, he was clearly visible. He saw Laramie walk out into the open, and then he heard Big Kev shout, 'Welcome back from the dead, Marshal Ford.'

A murmur rippled through the crowd as they looked up to see him. Shouts of disbelief reached his ears.

'Drop the rifle,' the man behind Ford said. 'Then the gunbelt.'

After he'd done so, the deputy asked, 'Now what?'

'We watch the entertainment.'

It was obvious to Laramie that they had been betrayed. He'd fully expected that it was a possibility and, judging by the smile on the kid's face, the young gunfighter was responsible. Oh, well, at least now he knew.

Bursts of anger erupted from the crowd at the subterfuge and some hurled abuse at the gunfighter; none of them would have had the spine to do so had he not been under the guns of the guards. A quick count from Laramie had their numbers at around a dozen. Not impossible by any stretch. Just interesting.

149

Big Kev walked forward a few more steps.

'I was trying to figure out what to do with you, Davis. After all, you are trying to put an end to my revenge. But young Jimmy here came up with an idea. He wants to test himself against your draw. So, there will be a change of plan. You and Jimmy will fight first and then Rivers and Polson.'

Laramie stared at the kid and saw the smile on his face.

'I was hoping I was wrong, kid,' he said. 'I guess I wasn't. Would have been a time I'd be happy to have been.'

'I can beat you, old man. I did it once, I can do it again.'

Laramie looked into the crowd for Ruby and saw the pale-faced woman standing beside Honey. He could read the fear she felt as she shook her head at him. He spoke out loud so everyone could hear, 'I'm sorry, Ruby.'

'I hope he kills you, you son of a bitch,' she hissed, but it was the fear talking.

Laramie turned to face the kid, who'd moved to one side, away from Big Kev. Not far from the man from St Louis were Red Rivers and the two guards. The gunfighter locked eyes with Rivers and an unspoken message passed between them. Rivers gave a slight nod to tell Laramie he was ready.

Next, he lifted his gaze to look at Ford. The man with him still had a gun pointed in the deputy's direction but he'd moved forward.

'Are you ready, old man?' Jimmy asked confidently.

'Or are you still enjoying your final moments? I don't mind waiting a little longer.'

A chuckle ran through those who'd come to town with the kid. Laramie looked at him and said in a calm voice, 'It's not too late, Jimmy. You can still walk away. I don't want to kill you.'

The kid chuckled. 'What makes you think *you* can kill me? You've had your day, old man. Time to give someone else a go.'

Laramie dropped his right hand to rest near the butt of his Peacemaker. He flexed his fingers and let his mind go blank, focusing on the kid in front of him.

A hush settled over the crowd and they waited for the killing to start. The kid wriggled his fingers, tickling his gun butt. Laramie watched, waiting. The wind blew along the street and then suddenly, out of a clear blue sky, came the sound of thunder rolling down from the mountains.

That was all it took.

Jimmy's expression changed to one of grim determination as his hand streaked toward his six-gun. His fingers curled around the butt and he brought it free of the leather in which it was encased. He smiled with satisfaction as he realized he'd never been so fast. The weapon started to level, his thumb had drawn back the hammer and his finger began to tighten on the trigger.

Thus, he couldn't believe it when the .45 calibre slug from Laramie's Colt smashed into his chest and forced all the air from his lungs.

Jimmy's eyes bulged and his jaw dropped. His knees buckled under him. He looked up at Laramie in wonderment. The gunfighter wasn't even looking at him. Why? That was when he realized that he was dying and there was no need for Laramie to concern himself with him. Jimmy's gun fell from his grasp and he died; a kid, not the man he'd thought he was.

After the slug burned deep into Jimmy's chest, Laramie switched his aim and pumped a second slug at the man on the roof beside Ford. Falling forward, the injured man cried out. He hit the edge of the building, and then cartwheeled onto the ground with a sickening thud. That gave the deputy a chance to grab his Winchester, which he scooped up and joined in the gun play.

Laramie's third shot punched into the guard beside Rivers. As the man fell, Rivers grabbed the guard's fully loaded six-gun from its holster with his left hand. He brought it around and up and shot the second guard in the side of the head. The bullet punched through and out the other side in a spray of crimson.

Scar Fletcher appeared from within the scattering crowd, six-gun in one hand and his sawn-off shotgun in the other. He aimed the small cannon at a shooter on the boardwalk outside of the saloon. The man, who was drawing a bead on Laramie, was about to fire when the shotgun roared and the double charge exploded from both barrels.

The impact almost cut the man in half. As it was, he was thrown back and disappeared through the saloon window.

Laramie glanced at Fletcher and nodded. The bounty hunter nodded back, then sought another target.

Rivers looked for Big Kev and saw him starting to moving quickly onto the boardwalk and into the saloon. He snapped off a shot and the hunk of lead chewed splinters from above the doorway.

On the roof, Ford levered a round into the Winchester and dropped a shooter on the saloon balcony opposite. The man jerked and crashed into the man next to him. He, in turn, pushed the wounded shooter away, causing him to crash through the rail.

The deputy snapped off another shot and the second man on the balcony died in a spray of blood when the .45-.75 slug tore a savage wound in his throat, severing an artery.

The man many had dubbed 'Legend' stood tall in the street, picking targets as they revealed themselves. Scar Fletcher came forward, firing as he went. More of Big Kev's men dropped where they stood, bodies shattered by lead slugs.

A loud shout made Laramie turn his head. Out of the carnage came Polson, a six-gun in each hand. The deputy brought up his guns to fire but both hammers fell on spent rounds. Laramie cursed at his vulnerability.

'Scar!' he snapped.

'I'm out too.'

'Shit!' Laramie snarled and started to reload.

Polson smiled wickedly as he lined up on the deputy's chest. Laramie knew he was going to be too late and went to dive to his left when a gunshot sounded and Polson fell forward. The killer hit the ground and didn't move. Behind him, however, holding a smoking Colt, was Tina, a shocked expression on her face.

She dropped the gun and ran, horrified at what she'd done, never having killed anyone before.

Slowly the tide of gunfire began to ebb. The bodies of Big Kev's killers lay strewn about the street. Eventually the firing stopped and an eerie silence, punctuated by the moans of the wounded, descended over the town. Laramie felt a dull burn in his left arm and looked down at the torn bloody sleeve. *Just a scratch*, he told himself.

'Laramie? You OK?'

He looked up and saw Ford standing on the roof, the Winchester in his hands. 'Yeah. You?'

'I'll live. Where's Rivers?'

Laramie stared at the street where he'd last seen the gunfighter. He wasn't there. The deputy shrugged. 'That's a good question.'

Then gunfire erupted from within the saloon.

CHAPTER 22

Bullets kicked up dirt at Rivers' boots and he snapped off a shot at the shooter under the awning. The gunfire was waning, and he saw Polson go down, shot from behind by Tina. He glanced at the saloon and smiled grimly. Bending down, he took the six-gun from the second dead guard and the key to his shackles, removed them and walked towards the saloon. There was one more man to kill.

He crashed through the batwing doors, to see people crouched behind tables and chairs, using them for cover just in case a stray slug came bursting through and found flesh.

At the sound of his entry, the barkeep popped his head up from behind the counter. Rivers stared hard at him and snarled, 'Where did the bastard go?'

'I – I don't know,' the barkeep stammered.

The gunfighter fixed his stare on a cowering man who had only the back of a chair between himself and oblivion. When he saw Rivers' harsh glare he paled, thinking he was about to die.

'Where did he go?'

The frightened man pointed at the doorway and said, 'Up the stairs.'

Rivers grunted and shook his head. He hurried towards the stairs, taking them two at a time until he reached the landing. Starting along the hall, he continued until he reached halfway. Suddenly a door flew open and Big Kev leaned out and blasted off two shots.

The bullets fizzed past Rivers' head and he ducked low. If the shots had been straight his action would have been way too late because he would be dead.

Rivers fired two of his own bullets at the opening and they chewed into the wall. Discarding the empty weapon, he thumbed back the hammer on the second gun. He moved forward to the doorway and peered into the room.

Big Kev rose from behind a messed-up bed and snapped off another shot. The bullet punched into the paper-thin wall across the hallway and into the room behind it.

The gunfighter fired again; he saw the bare mattress on the bed move from the bullet strike. While the killer's head was down, Rivers crossed the doorway to the other side and called out, 'It's over, you son of a bitch. Come on out.'

Big Kev fired two more shots. He'd shifted his aim this time and the bullets tore through the wall where the gunfighter had been standing. 'I think you missed, Kev. You've got nowhere to go. Come on out.'

The tinkle of shattering glass sounded as Big Kev's body crashed through the room's window. Rivers heard the thud of his body when it hit the balcony on the other side. The gunfighter hurried into the room. Through the smashed opening, he saw the bloodied figure of Big Kev stagger to his feet.

Rivers thumbed back the hammer on his six-gun and squeezed the trigger. Once, twice, three times.

Big Kev Riordan staggered and lurched like a drunk as each bullet hammered into his chest, the last of which drove him back against the balcony rail. With a dry crack, it gave way and the killer from St Louis disappeared over the edge.

Rivers climbed out onto the balcony and looked down to the street. Big Kev lay there on his back, unmoving. His left leg was twisted at an odd angle and the gun which had been in his hand now lay beside him. Then there was the large patch of red on his shirt. It was finally over.

'Are you OK, Red?' Laramie called up to him.

Rivers nodded. 'Yeah. I'm fine. Thanks.'

The gunfighter looked at the building across the street where Ford stood. They nodded at each other in acknowledgment.

They had pushed two tables together in the saloon and sat there with three bottles of whiskey which they were all pouring from; Laramie, Ford, Rivers, Fletcher, Honey, Cheyenne, and the other two girls. Two hours had passed since the final blazing showdown and they were happily using the alcohol to help the tension ease from them.

Many of those who'd come to Storm were now starting to leave. Ruby had claimed her son's body and loaded it into the wagon on which, full of vigour and seeking glory, he'd come into town.

'What will happen to the bodies?' Cara asked.

Fletcher cleared his throat. 'I'll be taking some of them with me. When Laramie approached me to help, he and I both knew at least three of them had paper out. There's possibly one or two more.'

'Don't you think. . . .'

'. . . that I should do something about them before they start stinking the place up?' the bounty hunter finished.

'Yes.'

'Ain't nothing I'm not used to.'

'What about you and Josh, Laramie? Where to from here?'

Laramie shrugged. 'To wherever the next case takes me I suppose.' He glanced at Ford sitting beside Cheyenne. 'Josh, on the other hand, might be due a few days off.'

Ford gave him a wry smile. 'Yeah, to recover from where you shot me.'

'I'm sure your nurse will take good care of you,' Laramie pointed out.

Cheyenne blushed and rested her head on Ford's shoulder. 'I'm sure I can.'

'I can't believe you're actually going to do it,' Honey said. 'I wish I could get away from it.'

'What's stopping you?' Rivers asked.

Honey chuckled. 'A man for starters. Who's going to look at me after he finds out what I do?'

'It didn't stop Josh,' Cheyenne pointed out.

'I thought the same thing,' Rivers said. 'Yet I had four beauties ride clear across from Kansas to help me out.' He reached down and took her by the hand. 'Maybe Ford's not the only one.'

Laramie's chair scraped back and he came to his feet. 'That's it for me. I'm gone. Before I end up married or some such. You coming, Josh?'

Ford rose from his seat and Cheyenne followed his move. 'I guess so.'

Rivers joined them and held out his hand. 'Thanks for your help, Laramie, Josh. If you ever need a man to help you out of a fix, just holler.'

Laramie took the hand and said, 'I will. Take care, Red.'

Ford slapped him on the shoulder. 'Glad we could help out, Red.'

Ford and Cheyenne started towards the batwings and Laramie heard her say, 'Can I ride your horse?'

'My horse? No.'

'Why not?'

'No.'

'Josh. . . .'

'No.'

'Oh, you're frustrating.'

They disappeared outside and Laramie shook his head. 'I hope it's not like that all the way back to Helena.'

Rivers chuckled. 'Be seeing you, Laramie.'

'You too, Red.'

Laramie followed Ford and Cheyenne from the saloon. When he reached the boardwalk, he watched them holding hands, walking along the street. He smiled. 'What the hell.'